Sex, Gore, & Millipedes

Sex, Gore, and Millipedes is published by Dragon's Roost Press.

A Youthful Heart originally appeared in *Fear's Accomplice 2,* by NoodleDoodle Productions, 2014
Appetites original appeared in *Slaughter House, Serial Killer Edition*, volume 3, by Sirens Call Publications, 2012
Dead Set on Vengeance originally appeared on *Cheapjack Pulp*, 2015
Danger's Balls originally appeared in *Morbid Metamorphosis*, by Lycan Valley Press, 2016
Impure Breed originally appeared in *Death Awaits Horror*, by Harren Press, 2013
Stiffed (with Kerry Lipp) originally appeared in *Life of the Dead*, by Martinus Press, 2014
The Grunt originally appeared in *Demonic Visions 2*, edited by Chris Robertson, 2013
The Mummy's Curves originally appeared in *On Devils and Deviants* by Crowded Quarantine Press, 2014
Upping the Production Values originally appeared in *Creepy Campfire Stories (for grown-ups)*, by EMP Publishing, 2015
What Little Boys are Made Of originally appeared in *HorrorAddicts.net* 2014
Bed Bugs, Fuck Bunny, and Starter Home are original material to this publication

Printed in the United States of America

First Printing, 2017

ISBN-13: 978-0-9988878-0-7
ISBN-10: 0-9988878-0-3

Dragon's Roost Press
207 Gardendale
Ferndale, MI 48220

http://thedragonsroost.net/styled-3/index.html

2017

Sex, Gore, & Millipedes

by Ken MacGregor

DEDICATION

For Brian Lillie, who told me to stop sending him scripts already and to go find a publisher or something.

TABLE OF CONTENTS

Acknowledgments

I'd very much like to thank, first and foremost, all the publishers who were kind of enough to give me a chance early in my career. In particular, I'd like to thank Gloria (Retired), Julianne and Nina over at Sirens Call Publications; their eZine was my very first time appearing with an actual publisher. It's been nearly six years since I began submitting stories, and I've learned so much in that time. I look back on my early work and shake my head at all the mistakes I used to make. It boggles the mind that I sold anything at all back then. So, thank you, to those who gave me a starting point. You guys rock.

Next, I'd like to thank Kerry Lipp, my sometime collaborator, and friend, who was kind enough to say, "Absolutely, man!" when I asked if I could add "Stiffed" to this collection. It was the first thing we wrote together. Since then, we've written another short story, and a novel (due out soon from Sirens Call Publications). I don't know if I could write with other people, but Kerry and I have a blast.

Next up is Jessica McHugh, a damn fine writer, who does it all, from kids' stuff to erotic horror. And, she does it well. She dropped a phrase in conversation that I adored, and I wanted to make it the title of my next collection. She told me to "Go for it!" so I did. (Thanks, Jess. I believe "Sex, Gore & Millipedes" lives up to its name.) If you like this book, go out and buy hers. You won't regret it.

I'd like to thank Marc and Joe over at Blood Bound Books. They rejected my story, "Starter Home" from the extreme horror anthology, DOA III. I had a story in DOA II, and really wanted to get in the third one. I didn't. However, here I was, with a 7100 word, twisted, disturbing story, and I thought, "Hey. I have some other really sick shit…let's put them all together in a book!" So, while I'm a little disappointed that I didn't make the cut for their antho, these guys were the catalyst that became the book in your hands. So, I appreciate them.

My editor, Michael Cieslak, and Dragon's Roost Press, for taking a chance on a collection of stories that is just about guaranteed to piss some people off. I appreciate, not only the vote of confidence, but also the darkly funny friendship we've developed over the last few years.

Lastly, I'd like to thank you, the reader, adventurous soul that you are, for picking up this book. I hope you find it entertaining, surprising, disturbing, and fun. If something in here really bothers you, and stays with you, worming its way into your mind, and keeping you up at night…good.

SEX, GORE, & MILLIPEDES

An Introduction

Hi. I'm Ken MacGregor, and I'm a pretty sick fuck. Just wanted to be up front with that, because if you keep reading, you're pretty likely to say, "Holy crap! This guy is a sick fuck! Why didn't somebody tell me?" Well, there you go. I've warned you. If you keep reading, that's on you, buddy. Of course, I hope you do, but I'll understand if you don't. This kind of thing isn't for everyone.

I *want* to bother you, to upset you, to trigger you. If you can't handle it, then by all means, put this book down and find something less disturbing to read.

But, for those of you who are into it, welcome. You are my people. Enjoy the wild, twisted, sick fucking ride.

Each of the fourteen stories in this book are designed to shock, to disturb, to titillate, to make your guts clench — sometimes at once. I set out to push the readers' boundaries, to shove you off the platform of your comfort zone and into the path of the speeding train of my fiction.

I would like to introduce you to some folks I created. Some of them are kind, thoughtful and caring; some are cruel, cold and heartless. And, I hurt most of them. I kill some, usually very slowly. And you? You get to watch. You get to sit on the sidelines of my game of cruelty, on the front row: the blood-spatter seats.

So, crack the spine (see what I did there?) and see what the darkness in my mind has vomited forth for your reading pleasure. I hope you are comfortable, because you won't be for long.

Ken MacGregor

2016

Fuck Bunny

"Happy Birthday-slash-Easter, Jessica!"

Her dad stepped away from the table, revealing her present. Jess cocked her head to the left and twisted her lip sideways.

"Um. It's a giant rabbit."

Her dad nodded, grinning like he used to when she was little and got her math problems right on the first try.

"Solid chocolate. Two feet tall. Weighs sixty-five pounds. Just like the ones my dad used to get. Remember?"

How could she forget? The rabbit, which must have cost a fortune, was handmade and delivered every year just before Easter. On those rare years when her birthday was on Easter week, Jess would be allowed the first bite. It was a tiny, melty chunk of heaven in her mouth.

"I didn't think anyone made these anymore," she said now. "That place Poppy used to get them died with the owners, right?"

"Yeah. I found a guy." Eyebrow waggle. I know something you don't expression. She could read him so well. That's all the information she was going to get.

"Well, this is certainly a surprise. Thanks, Dad. It's going to take me years to eat this thing."

He draped an arm over her shoulder. She leaned her head on him out of habit more than anything.

"You be sure to save me some." He laughed his big, fake donkey bray. The one that hurt her ears. The one she never liked.

When she was alone (her dad was the only visitor on her birthday), Jess pulled the ends of the ribbon holding the cellophane shut at the top of her present. She peeled the crinkling plastic back and down to reveal the smooth, glossy brown rabbit.

The distinguishing features, beyond the obvious, were seven whiskers (four on the right, three on the left) and a polka-dot bowtie.

She leaned in close and inhaled. The smell caused spit to pool around her tongue.

"Mm. I can't wait to eat you, little bunny."

Its chocolate nose twitched. All seven whiskers snapped out straight, leaving indents in the rabbit's face where they had been. Its tiny, smiling mouth opened. From it, a four-inch, ropy, chocolate *something* snaked out. It looked like a cross between a human tongue and a barbed cat penis.

"I was just gonna say the same thing about you."

Her jaw hung slack for a few seconds. She snapped it shut.

"You can *talk?*"

"Yeah," he said, with a tiny, chocolate leer, "but that's the least of my mouth's talents."

Jessica leaned her chin on her palms, elbows propped on the table. After the initial shock of the rabbit speaking to her, she found it (*him*, she supposed; between the chocolate legs, she could make out testicles and the tube-sheath of a penis) more fascinating than anything.

"How is it that you can talk?"

He shrugged his tiny, chocolate shoulders.

"I don't know. Magic? Mad scientist? I didn't even know I could, until you spoke to me. Then, I suddenly realized I wanted to respond. Mostly, because you're pretty much smokin' hot. For a human, anyway."

"Should I be insulted?"

He raised a chocolate eyebrow.

"You were gonna *eat* me. And, you're offended by me saying you're hot for a human."

She lifted her head and scowled at him.

"You were gonna eat me, too." The bunny grinned.

"Oh. *Oh.* Really?" Jessica's face grew hot.

"Why don't you climb on up here and lift your skirt and find out?"

She looked around, even though she knew she was alone.

"Seriously?"

"Yup."

For a long time, she sat and stared at the rabbit. The idea certainly had appeal. She liked oral. Who doesn't? But, this was just weird. Finally, it occurred to her that right here was a once-in-a-lifetime opportunity. No one else in history had probably ever had a large, solid chocolate bunny go down on them.

She reached under her skirt and shimmied out of her underwear. They puddled around her ankles and she stepped out of them, fighting a bit with the left side as it caught on her heel.

"Okay," she said, climbing atop the table in what she hoped was a sexy way. "I'm game."

The bunny's tongue was quick and agile. Within minutes, Jess writhed, forcing her hips not to buck, to stay there, where the tongue was. The rough edges, the tiny barb-things she had seen earlier, were almost painful at first, but soon she stopped feeling them. She wondered briefly (in a moment when the bunny paused, and she could think) if she was just used to it, or if it was melting. She felt like her cunt was a hundred and ten degrees Fahrenheit.

She came nine times. Definitely a record. When she had caught her breath, she lifted her head and looked at the rabbit. His face looked mildly distorted with a few whiskers missing, but he smiled.

"Yummy."

Jess raised her skirt and pushed herself up on shaking elbows. The insides of her thighs were smeared with melted chocolate. One thin whisker was plastered to her groin. She peeled it off and ate it. The bunny shuddered.

"I hurt you," she said.

"I don't mind."

She leaned her head back, dangling her hair over the table. She laughed, impromptu.

"That was amazing. Nobody has ever made me feel like that. Thank you."

The rabbit was silent. She pushed herself up to a sitting position and regarded him. He was smiling at her. His one remaining whisker quivered.

"You're welcome. I enjoyed giving you pleasure. Now, it's my turn. I'm gonna fuck you 'til you go insane."

He spread his muscular, chocolate legs to reveal two inches of shining penis proudly thrusting from the sheath between his legs.

She frowned.

"Um. With *that*?"

It retracted a bit under her scrutiny. The bunny looked down in shame. His voice was almost a whisper.

"It is all I have."

She pouted at him sympathetically. Still warm from his administrations, still wet in fact, she shrugged.

"How about your ears? They're pretty big. And, after, I can blow you."

"You want to put my ears in your…"

"One anyway. I think both at once would probably hurt."

He wiggled his ears experimentally.

She watched the movement with widened eyes.

"I mean," he said, "I guess that would be okay. My ears aren't exactly erogenous zones, but I suppose I can wait a little longer for my own release. You'll really blow me after?"

She licked her lips and crossed her heart.

"Promise."

He grinned.

"Lady, you have yourself a deal."

She got on her knees to peel off her shirt. She slid on the linen placemat, almost pulling a muscle, and tossed it off the table. She wore no bra over her B-cup breasts. They jiggled slightly when released. The rabbit watched intently as her nipples hardened in the breeze from the ceiling fan.

She unzipped her skirt and pushed it down to her knees. Flipping herself over, she slid it off the rest of the way. She smiled at the bunny, her eyes dancing with lustful mischief.

"What?" he asked.

She shrugged a little. She idly rotated the ends of her nipples with the tips of her middle fingers.

"It's weird, that's all. I'm about to fuck the ears of a chocolate Easter bunny. I should be freaking out, wondering if maybe I've lost my mind."

"But, you're not?"

"Nope. Mostly, I'm just horny as hell."

The rabbit licked his lips with his new shorter and smoother tongue.

"Works for me," he said. His lisp was barely noticeable.

She stood. There was a wooden *thump-thump-thump*.

"Ow." Holding her head with one hand, she pulled the chain three times to shut the fan all the way off. She laughed and rubbed the sore spot. "That was pretty dumb."

A squelching sound make her look down. The rabbit had forced his big legs to separate from his body and was shuffling toward her. She stood still, feet wide apart and waited for him. When he was directly under her, she lowered herself just enough to feel the tip of one ear against her labia.

Holding it with one hand, she rolled her hips forward and then back, sliding the ear along the edge of her slit. On the way back, it bumped her clitoris. It was, well, delicious.

Sliding a finger inside herself, she licked it.

"Oh wow. I taste great with chocolate."

"Everything does," he said.

She eased down over the ear. It felt strange, but good. It stretched her in ways a penis wouldn't, but it didn't hurt. It was different. It was nice.

Holding his other ear for balance, she rocked her pelvis a little to one side, then the other. Inside her, the ear twitched, and she gasped. Soon, her thighs shook, her toes curled against the table, and she clenched around that ear in a head-back, teeth-clenching orgasm.

"Oh. My. God."

She slid up and off of him, bumping her head on the stationary fan blade and snorting laughter. She dropped to a squat, one hand down for balance. The other covered her mouth.

"Oh no."

"What?" the bunny asked.

"Your ear. It's all bent and melted. I'm so sorry."

He looked up and moved his ears into view. The left was fine, save for some shallow finger marks, but the right looked more carrot than ear.

"Hm. Well, it *was* pretty hot in there." He grinned at her. "So, now it's, um, my turn?"

"Uh huh."

Jess eased herself off the table. Her leg muscles were still shaky. She cupped her hands around his butt, fingers laced behind his puffy, chocolate tail, and pulled him to the edge. She got on her knees.

After playing with the bunny's balls for a few seconds, his prick slid out of its sheath. She took it in her mouth and massaged the underside with her tongue.

"Mmm."

She worked him in and out, tongue playing along the tiny shaft. She could feel his little paws on her head, kneading in her hair.

The rabbit's breath came faster. He jerked in her mouth. His whole solid chocolate body got even stiffer. Her mouth filled with hot, sweet syrup and she drank it down.

She looked up at him, a triumphant grin on her face.

He touched her cheek. He was still trying to catch his breath.

"I think I love you."

She laughed.

"Thanks. You're very sweet. Literally. Listen, bunny. I need a shower. I really, really need a shower. You okay for a few minutes?"

"Lady, I have never been more okay in my entire life."

She sat at the table in her old terrycloth robe which had once been yellow, soft and fluffy, and was now pale no-color and a bit stiff. Jessica piled her hair in a towel turban atop her head. A slight welt shone pink above her eye where the ceiling fan had tagged her.

"I don't know anything about you," the rabbit said.

She laughed. "Jesus, that's so cliché."

"Sorry," he said.

"No. I'm sorry. That was mean of me. Really, there's not much to tell. I work, I come home, have a glass or three of wine, and watch Netflix. Once in a while, I hang out with friends. Even more rarely, I go on dates. For 29, I'm pretty boring."

"Twenty-nine today. Happy birthday."

"Thanks. Yeah. It's been pretty good all right. Multiple orgasms: best gift ever."

He chuckled. His good ear twitched. She noticed and her tongue touched her lip.

"Well," she said, focusing on his eyes again, "what about you, my friend? I'm sure your story is way more interesting than my own. I mean, you're a magic, talking, chocolate Easter bunny. Wow."

He shrugged.

"Well, seeing as how I've only been conscious for a couple hours now, and most of that has been spent in your mouth and cunt, I'd have to say I have led a pretty amazing life."

"That's an ugly word."

"'Life?'"

"No. 'Cunt.'"

"It's not ugly at all. It's a powerful word. One syllable. Hard consonants on both ends. Undeniable. By contrast, the word 'vagina' means 'sheath', a place for a man to put his metaphorical sword. But, 'cunt' is the whole thing: the hot, wrinkled, furry, stinky, wonderful place between a woman's legs. It's fucking beautiful."

She peeled the towel from her head and combed her hair with her fingers. Setting the towel on her lap, she cocked her head to one side.

"Maybe I should start using 'cunt' in conversation. Probably raise some eyebrows."

He nodded.

"Probably. It's good to shake things up. People are too complacent."

"You know a hell of a lot for a chocolate rabbit who's only been conscious for half a day."

He smirked.

"I'm a talking chunk of candy who ejaculates hot syrup. And, what's surprising to you is that I'm well-informed?"

She took a deep breath and let it out of her nose.

"Frankly, it's all pretty surprising." Her eyes suddenly widened. "I want to try something."

He started to ask what, but before he could get it out, she reached over and broke off part of his melted, mangled ear. She popped it in her mouth. He stared at her, jaw hanging.

"Sorry. So good though."

The bunny nodded.

"If it gives you pleasure, my love, it's fine. I would do anything for you. You have captured my tiny, chocolate heart."

On Wednesday, Jessica's father stopped by. He brought an inexpensive, but decent bottle of red wine.

"Goes with chocolate," he said. "I'm assuming there's still some left?"

She nodded.

"A little, yeah. He's in the fridge."

His brows shot up.

"'He?'"

She flushed and shrugged.

"I decided he was a boy bunny. Whatever. Open the wine."

He found the corkscrew in its usual drawer. The cork came out with a soft *pop*. While the bottle breathed, he pulled two glasses out by the stems. He *tsked* over the dishes left in the sink.

"How was the rest of your birthday?"

She looked away, swallowing.

"Good."

She poured them each a glass.

Her father opened the fridge. Behind him, she tensed, fingers clutching the bottle until they hurt.

"Hey. You ate the whole head? I wanted an ear."

"Sorry. I had to. He wouldn't shut up."

He laughed and pulled the rabbit carcass from the fridge. Setting it on a chopping block, he pulled the cleaver from its place. Taking careful aim, he lopped off one of the back feet. As he picked it up, he snorted.

"Would you look at that? They gave this rabbit balls. I guess it *is* a boy. I'm a little surprised it doesn't have a penis, too."

"It did. I ate that."

He eyed his daughter, mouth hanging open a bit.

"That's messed up, honey."

She nodded.

"You have no idea."

He cut the foot in two and handed her half. They ate and washed it down with wine. They were both staring at the headless centerpiece. Jessica sighed and he met her eyes.

"I think next year, for my birthday, I'd rather go to a movie or something."

A Youthful Heart

"It's not pretty, but it works." The old man stood very close and smiled. His teeth were yellow and his breath smelled of pipe tobacco and spearmint. His skin was like ancient parchment: pale and textured.

Bianca made a noncommittal noise and set down the portable radio. Browsing further down the driveway, she moved away from him.

A stack of DVDs caught her eye; she pulled them forward one at a time, looking at each cover. Most of them were Bruce Willis and Jackie Chan films: actions and comedies, which were not things she watched.

"Those belonged to my son, Brian." the old man said. "He passed away ten years ago."

"I'm sorry," Bianca said. She pulled her hand away from the DVDs and wiped it on her pant leg. The old man watched her do it.

"Death freaks you out, huh?"

"A little. I think everyone is afraid of death, at least to some degree." Her cheeks flushed and she looked at a toaster, pushing the lever up and down twice.

"Sure. Most folks. Though, at my age, it's not so scary; it's probably a proximity thing." He paused. "I can see I've made you uncomfortable. Forgive me."

"Not at all," she said. "It's fine."

The old man's eyes twinkled.

"Tell you what," he said. "I'll let you have anything on this table for free. Not the stuff over there; I plan to make some real money on those things."

She looked over the items around the DVDs and the toaster. A set of two blue glass candlesticks held her interest for a moment, but then something caught her eye. Tucked behind a shoebox full of porcelain figurines in various states of disrepair was a jar. It was the old fashioned kind used to preserve fruit. Picking it up, she tilted it and looked inside. Semi-transparent liquid sloshed aside to reveal what looked like a human heart. The jar was cold in her hand.

She turned to the old man.

"What is this?"

"This is a sheep's heart, miss. A souvenir from my days as a biology teacher. That the thing you want?"

Bianca nodded. The old man cocked his head to the side and pursed his thin lips.

"Been a long time since I gave a pretty lady my heart." He grinned. Bianca smiled politely back and also bought both candlesticks for a dollar.

In the living room of her one-bedroom apartment, Bianca set the new candlesticks a foot apart on the mantle over her gas fireplace. She set the jar with the heart between them and went to look for candles. She found a four-pack of tall, white tapers in the utility drawer in the kitchen and grabbed two of them. She worked them into the too-small candlestick holders; some wax flaked onto the mantle and she swept it into her hand.

Leaving the candles unlit, Bianca preheated the oven and pulled the double-cheese pizza out of the freezer. On Saturdays, she didn't cook. She peeled away the plastic and put all the errant bits of cheese back on the pie. It looked not so much like something to eat as the drawing of a first-grader. The oven beeped and she slid the pizza onto the top rack; she set the timer and threw herself onto the couch. The copy of the Smithsonian magazine lay open to the article she had been reading; she picked it up and looked at the pictures of melting glaciers. Her eyes slipped off the text, drawn to the fireplace with its new adornments.

Red heart; white wall; blue candlesticks: *patriotic*. Returning to the utility drawer, she found a lighter; she trimmed the candle wicks with scissors and lit them. The glow from the flames cast a warm light into the fluid in the jar. The organ inside had turned a deeper red and its contours were easier to see.

Bianca touched the jar with her fingertips. It was much warmer now. In the fluid, the heart seemed to move a tiny bit. She pulled away, but then stopped.

"I must have bumped it," she said. Behind her, the oven timer chimed. "Pizza's up."

Dinner was served on a paper plate; she didn't do dishes on Saturday either. She ate half the pie and put the rest in a Pyrex container in the fridge. She started water for tea and dropped a bag of chamomile into a mug, looping the string around the handle.

Turning on the TV, she surfed for a while, only staying on a given channel for a second or two. She stopped on a movie: *Hudson Hawk* starring Bruce Willis. She watched it until the kettle shrieked. A long time ago, Bianca had seen the film, but barely remembered it; this time, she laughed out loud and leaned forward over her tea cup. When the credits rolled, she was still chuckling. Blowing out the candles, she yawned and patted the jar. Wisps of grey smoke snaked up toward the ceiling.

"G'night, sheep's heart. You are mine, and I shall call you Brian," she said. She rinsed her mug and put it in the dishwasher. Turning out the kitchen light, she found her way to her room in the dark.

Shortly after one am, she woke up to the throes of a bed-shaking orgasm. She rode it out, clutching the sheets with both hands, sweat pouring off of her. When she had caught her breath, Bianca opened her eyes and laughed.

"Wow. That must have been one hell of a dream." She fell back to sleep smiling.

When the sun slanted through the blinds, she woke to the smell of fresh-brewed coffee. She tried to remember if she had set it up the night before. Pulling on her silk robe, she headed to the kitchen, scratching her belly and yawning. The black machine on the counter was full of fresh, hot coffee. Shrugging, she poured herself some.

"Early onset of dementia, I suppose. Symptoms are forgetting you made coffee and talking to yourself. Mmmm. Good coffee. Thanks, unconscious self."

In the bathroom mirror, she stared at her untamed hair. She snorted laughter.

"Looks like I had a man in my bed."

She ran her fingers through her hair. They got caught in the snarls, making her wince. Once she was showered and dressed, Bianca went to church. She wasn't a believer; she went for the sense of community. She also liked the choir, though they sang with more passion than skill. This Sunday, the reverend's sermon was tepid and forgettable, but the sunlight through the tall, stained glass windows was breathtaking. Trade-offs. A young couple sat in the pew in front of her. The woman's hair was recently styled; she wore pearl studs in her ears. Next to her, with the high and tight haircut preferred by Marines, the man sat rigidly, jaw clenching and unclenching over and over. He seemed furious that he had to be there.

Back home, Bianca changed into sweatpants and a Tweety Bird T-shirt. She made an egg salad sandwich and wolfed it down. She loaded the washing machine and started it. She walked around the house, collecting the clutter that accrued throughout the week and put everything away. She swept the kitchen and bathroom floors, flipped the clothes into the dryer and did a thirty minute yoga video.

When she hit stop on the DVD player, *Drunken Monkey* was playing on TV. She lifted her shirt to wipe sweat from her face and stood on the mat watching Jackie Chan. Soon, she was laughing and cheering for the goofy, lovable hero.

When the movie slowed for exposition, she opened the fridge for a bottle of water. When the door was wide, a cool blast of air pushed against her, flattening the clothes to her body. Gooseflesh rippled all over and her nipples pushed against her shirt. The cold seemed to penetrate all the way through. Her hand tightened on the bottle; the plastic crinkled. The feeling lingered for a few seconds after the breeze stopped.

"That was weird."

She closed the fridge and twisted the cap off the water. She drained half of it. Back in the living room, silly kung fu was in full swing. Sitting on the couch, she crossed her legs and set the bottle next to her between the cushions. The background music in the movie had a steady rhythmic pulse to it; her foot kept time on the floor.

The TV shut itself off. She stared at the screen and pressed her lips together. The drum part of the music was still playing, thumping along slow and steady like a metronome. It wasn't coming from the set though. Closing her eyes, she tilted her head, slowly turning it. When she had pinpointed the source, she opened her eyes.

On the mantle, the heart beat; the flexing muscle made the liquid slosh against the top of the jar.

"Brian?"

The heart stopped. She held her breath. Her own heart beat fast in her chest. After almost a minute of silence, she got up and went to her room. She came out dressed and splashed water on her face. She sketched eyeliner on her bottom lids and snagged her keys from the hook. Shooting one last look at the jar, she left.

By the time she got to the old man's yard, the sun was close to the horizon. The tables were still out, but most of the stuff was gone. From the dim garage, the old man emerged; there was color in his cheeks, though he wasn't winded. He stopped when he saw her.

"All sales are final."

"That wasn't a sheep heart, was it?"

The old man looked at her for a long moment without speaking, his jaw clenched.

"All sales are final."

She nodded. She looked away, down the street where a child was counting loudly, leaning face-first against a tree. Other children scattered and hid; they wore insane grins. Bianca looked once more at the old man, shook her head and turned to go. She watched her feet as she walked home, avoiding the sidewalk cracks by long habit.

When she put the key in the lock, an electric jolt shot up her arm. It was mild and didn't hurt, but she jumped. Gathering folds of her blouse, Bianca used it to turn the key. She went in and closed the door by leaning on it.

The water bottle was sticking up between the couch cushions where Bianca had left it. For several seconds, she stared at it. Movement caught her eye.

The heart was beating.

Behind her ribs, her own heart pulsed a half-second off at first, but then started keeping time with the one in the jar. Though the windows were closed, a cool breeze picked up in the room. It blew her hair back and made her blink. The soft wind pushed against her and she pressed her back into the door, palms flat against the wood.

Feeling a tug, she looked down. Her jacket's zipper tab was sticking straight out, pulling the fabric from her body. Her eyes went wide as the zipper crawled down and snapped off at the end.

A gust pushed the jacket off her shoulders and down her arms. She didn't move to stop it; she took in quick gulps of air. Though the draft was cool on her skin, heat was building between her legs. Pushing her toes into her heels, she kicked off her shoes.

She pulled her shirt over her head and slid down her sweat pants.

Slipping a hand into the waistband of her underwear, she felt how wet she was and gasped.

The two hearts in the room pounded together. Other, unseen hands caressed her skin: her neck; collarbone; the swells of her breasts; her buttocks.

Then, he was inside her. Leaning against the door, she thrust her hips out and back, riding her invisible lover. He was the perfect size, the ideal shape.

The heart beat faster on the mantle. The jar shook with it. Her own heart blazed in her chest; she cried out and her legs went rigid, her toes pointed and she collapsed to the floor.

Bianca's heart gradually slowed. The heart on the mantle had stopped. She caught her breath, crawled to the couch and drank the tepid water in the bottle all at once. She levered herself onto the cushions with shaky arms and legs.

"Could have bought me dinner first."

Sitting at her desk the next day, she gazed through her monitor, seeing nothing. The hand falling on her shoulder made her jump.

"Sorry," Gwen said, holding up her hands palms out. "Party too hard this weekend?" She smiled at her own joke.

"No. I just have a lot on my mind. I'll stop woolgathering, I promise."

"No problem. I wanted to let you know the Mackenzie case is wrapped up. I already filed it."

Bianca thanked her and returned her attention to the case she was working on. A small business had burned to the ground, and arson was certain. What was less sure was whether the owner had set it, paid someone else to set it or was himself the victim. The evidence was pointing toward the latter, but it was her job to find the truth. She had an excellent track record of doing just that.

The black plastic phone on her desk rang. She stared at the number on the display for a moment before picking up the receiver. It was the landline at her house. She put it to her ear without saying anything.

It was the steady rhythm of a beating heart. She pressed the phone tight to her head. Her eyes darted around, but no one was near her. She whispered into the mouthpiece.

"Brian?"

Her only answer was the thump-thump getting faster. Her heart sped up with it. She pressed her thighs together under her desk.

"I can't do this now. I'm at work." She hissed the words into the phone, but she didn't hang up.

The unmistakable hot, wet feel of a tongue was on her, as if her underwear didn't exist. The phantom licked, flicked and teased her. Gripping the edge of the desk with her free hand, she listened to the heart on the phone. She spread her legs and closed her eyes. Pleasure washed over her. Her knuckles were white on the handset. Her office chair tilted back, and her feet shot out and she did her best to be silent as the orgasm rocked her world.

The phone clicked and the beating heart was replaced by a dial tone. Letting both hands fall, she could still hear the faint tone at her side. She opened her eyes.

Standing next to her, eyes wide and mouth open, Gwen held a file folder limp in one hand. Bianca sat up straight and hung up the phone. She was about to speak when the aftershock hit and she shuddered and caught her breath. She touched her upper lip with her tongue and smiled.

"Wow."

"I don't, that is, did you, I mean, there is a policy about taking personal calls at your desk, Bianca."

"That one was personal all right." She laughed. She looked at the file in the other woman's hand. "Gwen, I'm sorry, but whatever that is has to wait. I'm taking the rest of the day off."

Pushing past an unmoving Gwen, she snagged her jacket off the edge of her cubicle wall. She tugged it on as she walked through the door.

She detoured a few blocks on the way home, pulling up to the old man's house. Taking the place of long tables in the driveway was a lime green classic Mustang. The vanity plate read 68STANG. It was in near-mint condition; the only obvious flaw was a small tear in the rag top, patched with black duct tape.

"My favorite's the sixty-four, but I couldn't find one at the right price." The old man stepped off his porch, wiping wet hands on a small teal towel.

"When I was seventeen, I had a seventy-two hard top," she said. "But, it was half made of rust and never started on the first try." She looked at him, tilting her head to one side.

"What?"

"Did you start dyeing your hair? It looks darker." The old man grinned.

"You like it?"

She shrugged and the man's grin died.

"Makes you look a lot younger."

"Did you just come by to talk about my looks, or did you need something?" He tucked the towel in the back of his belt and hooked his thumbs in his front pockets.

"The heart, um," she started. She blushed. "It beats."

"Yeah. Hearts do that."

"Not when they're in jars, usually." The old man shrugged. "Also, when it beats, things happen." She looked away and down. Her flush spread to her neck and ears.

"What kind of things?"

She snapped her gaze to his. Something in his tone made it sound like he knew exactly what happened when the heartbeat.

"I don't know why I'm even talking to you." Turning away, she hurried to her car.

"Hey." He said it softly, but his voice carried. With her hand on the door, she turned to face him. "You're the one who keeps coming back."

She got in her car without another word. She racked the gear shift into drive and floored it.

Ten minutes later, she had to pull over; invisible, yet familiar hands were stroking her. Heat and pressure slid inside Bianca and filled her. It stopped just short of being painful. She undid her seatbelt and thumbed the hazards button. Pulling up her skirt, she slid a hand inside her underwear. Her fingers moved across her own flesh, warm and swollen. Closing her eyes, she shut out the world.

The rhythmic clicking of the hazards evolved into a heartbeat. Lifting her hips, she moved her hand lower. She wrapped it around the thick shaft sliding in and out of her. It was wet from her and she could feel its pulse in her hand. It slid within her grasp, working its way into her until it could go no further.

Leaning forward, she stroked the invisible shaft. It kept going, long as a snake. Sliding it along, further out from herself, her hand hit the steering column. Her eyes snapped open and she shot a quick look around; cars drove by, ignoring her.

The movement inside her never ceased. The hazard lights beat on the dash, red pulsing heartbeat matching her own. Closing her eyes again, she surrendered herself to the pleasure. As she climaxed, the shaft in her hand stiffened and pulsated.

When she had caught her breath, she straightened her skirt and ran her fingers through her hair. As her hand passed her face, she could smell herself on her fingers. Something else was there, too: a sharp, musky man-smell that made her head jerk away. She shook it off, blinked and started driving with a smile plastered on her face.

Stopping for a bottle of wine, she walked stiffly through the store aisles. Choosing a twelve-dollar bottle of red, she stood in line behind a huge man who reeked of cigarette smoke. She held back a few feet from him; his odor hung in the air at the counter after he was gone. The man at the register was fortyish, pale and thin. He licked his lips and looked at her tits, not bothering to be subtle. Sighing, she held out a twenty.

He sniffed the air and his lips stretched over a crooked-toothed smile. One of his incisors was capped with gold. The man snatched her hand, held it to his face and licked her middle finger. She pulled back, but he held on with a grip too strong to break.

"You taste good."

She bit down hard, grinding her teeth. Her middle finger tapped on the wrist of the one who held her. *Tuh-tum, tuh-tum* on the man's pulse. Inside her chest, her own heart paced the finger.

The man's grin fell and his eyes narrowed, but he didn't let her go.

"What are you doing?"

Tuh-tum, tuh-tum. She could see the pulse in the man's throat keeping time. He opened his mouth but only air came out. She watched his eyes as she tap-tapped.

From inside her heart, a coldness grew. It spread out to fill her ribcage and flowed down into her pelvis. The cold was a living thing inside her, settling into her guts. Like a slingshot pulled to its limit, the cold shot from within her, out along her arm and into the man behind the counter.

The man's lips curled back from his gold tooth and the capillaries in both his eyes burst all at once. The pulse in his neck stopped. The hand holding Bianca's relaxed as the man crumpled to the floor.

Setting the twenty on the counter, Bianca grabbed the wine and turned to leave.

"Keep it," she said.

Behind the wheel of her car, her hand shook so hard she couldn't get the key in the ignition; after several tries, she threw the key ring on the floor in front of the passenger seat. Clenching her fists, she pushed her butt up and sat on her hands. After a long time, she got her body under control; she put her hands on the wheel and her foot on the brake. Frowning, she leaned over and grabbed the keys. She started the car and put it in gear. Foot on the brake, car unmoving, she looked at her own eyes in the rearview.

"I killed that man." Her eyes in the convex rectangle widened. "No. I didn't. Brian killed him. The ghost heart killed him."

Pulling out into traffic, she cut off a Honda Fit; the driver blared his little horn at her. Hitting the brakes hard, she waved and called out an apology. When the road was clear, she drove home.

Slamming the door behind her, she stormed to the fireplace. She leaned in and glared at the heart in the jar. It sat still and quiet in its liquid environment.

"You killed that man, didn't you? Somehow, through me, you killed him.

Right?"

A warm breeze blew up from the floorboards and caressed her legs, sliding between her thighs toward her groin.

"Knock it off."

She clamped her legs together and grabbed the jar with both hands. The breeze stopped and the temperature of the jar dropped ten degrees. She shivered, but held on.

"I don't know what this is, any of it," she said. "I mean, the sex is amazing, if *completely* weird, but you can't go around killing everyone who is an asshole to me. If we're going to make this work, you need to rein in your temper."

The jar warmed up in her hands. The heart started to beat, one beat every few seconds at first. The rate sped up. Her breathing sped up, too and her heart rate matched the one she held. In her hand, the jar grew almost hot. She sat on the floor and held the jar between her legs, tight to the crotch of her pants. Gasping from the heat, she pressed the jar to herself, grinding her pelvis against the glass.

Arching her back, she cried out as the orgasm shook her body. The jar was so hot. Her fingers were red and sore where they had touched it. She left it there and ran her hands under cold water, then drank several swallows from the tap.

When she came back out of the bathroom, the jar was in its place on the mantle again, between the blue candlesticks. With a wink and a grin, she leaned close.

"Make-up sex is my favorite."

She kissed the lid. Stripping her shirt off on the way, she went to shower. Wearing an extra-long T-shirt that came almost to her knees, she reemerged fifteen minutes later. She went to the kitchen and made a tuna sandwich. She ate it with a glass of milk while reading a four-month-old National Geographic. One of the articles was accompanied by the photo of a huge pile of skulls; she stared it for a long time.

Putting on clean clothes and sneakers, Bianca waved to the heart and went out. Her feet zoomed along the now familiar route and she found herself standing on the old man's front porch, finger poised over the doorbell button.

After several seconds, she pushed it. A faint tinkling sound came from within. A moment passed, then she heard footsteps and the door opened. A forty-something man looked at her. She didn't recognize him, though he was clearly a relation of the old man who lived there. He had the same eyes and cheekbones, the same chin.

"Um, hi. I was looking for, um, I'm sorry. It just occurred to me I never learned his name."

"Jacob," the man said. She smiled.

"Thank you. I'm Bianca. I bought some things at a yard sale and I've been back a couple times to, ah, talk about one of them. Is Jacob your dad? Is he home?"

"I'm Jacob."

Her face went hot and red.

"I'm sorry. I thought you meant the old man was Jacob."

The man grinned and she blanched. She knew that grin.

"That's right. I'm Jacob, when I'm old and when I'm not. I'm still me no matter what."

Heart thumping in her chest, she stepped back. Her heel edged over the top step and she almost lost her balance.

"You're getting younger. How are you doing that?"

"It's you, Bianca. You're making me younger."

"I don't understand."

He leaned toward her. She could smell pipe tobacco on his breath. He put his hands with their long fingers on her shoulders. She stiffened, but didn't pull away. He moved close and put his lips to her ear. His breath tickled her neck and she shivered.

"The heart, dear lady, is mine. When you climax, it feeds me, makes me younger. Also, it's a lot of fun."

"You're some kind of vampire."

He stepped back. He was frowning. Dropping his hands from Bianca, he shook his head.

"No, my dear. Vampires are make-believe. If you must label me, please use the term 'incubus.' It's not strictly accurate, but will suffice."

She opened her mouth, closed it, then opened it again. She said nothing. She turned away from Jacob and walked home again. Outside her door, she held the key in her hand and stared at the grain of the wood in front of her.

For five full minutes, she stayed like that, keys in hand, not opening her door.

She put the key in the lock, flinching for the electric shock that never came and went inside. Her home looked just as she left it. Looking at the heart in the jar, she frowned and let the breath out of her nose all at once.

"I have to go pee, and then you and I are going to have a serious talk."

Taking her time with washing her hands, she looked at herself in the mirror. She had picked up more than a few gray hairs in the last week or so.

"Has it only been a week?"

Her reflection didn't answer. She kept drying her hands long after all the water was gone. She folded the towel in half and hung it neatly on the rack. Putting her hand on the doorknob, she sighed once more and opened the door.

The heart beat in the jar, and the liquid sloshed a bit against the glass. Shea felt her own heart start to beat in time and she thumped herself on the chest with her fist and shook her head. Without looking at the mantle, she headed to the kitchen. She came out in a moment with a flat rubber circle with tiny bumps on one side.

"You know what this is, Brian? Or should I say 'Jacob'? It's really handy, you know. For opening jars that are stuck. I haven't had to use it in a while, but I think it's about time I did."

The heart in the jar pumped much faster and the sound reverberated off the walls and in her head. She advanced on the mantle, balancing the rubber circle in her hand.

The TV turned itself on; Bruce Willis was fighting for his life against an enormous man in an orange jumpsuit. Dramatic music and a thunderstorm punctuated the scene.

When she reached for the jar, the candles both burst into flame half a foot high. She flinched back, but the fire soon fell to a normal height and she grabbed the jar.

Ice covered it instantly and she dropped the jar, crying out. Taking her shirt off, she wrapped the cloth around her hand and turned the jar upright on the floor. She slammed the rubber disc onto the lid and gripped it with everything she had. Giving it a mighty twist, she opened the jar.

The rank, pungent smell of the biology lab hit her and she gagged and jerked away. The jar fell over and formaldehyde poured out onto the floor.

She crab-scrambled away from the mess, dropping the shirt and jar-opener. As she watched, the heart slipped out of the jar and lay beating on the floor.

On the TV, Bruce Willis was in a pool, trapped under a tarp and holding his breath.

The heart beat louder now, the sound drowned out the TV and everything else. It was all she could hear and she couldn't look away from the wet, pulsating organ on her living room floor.

In the kitchen, the refrigerator door flew open and banged into the wall. The bottles of condiments on the shelf rattled; the ketchup fell to the floor, bounced and was still. Cold air from the fridge poured out and enveloped her. Icy fingers ripped open the snap of her jeans and pulled the zipper down.

Grabbing the denim with both hands, she tried to hold up her pants, but they were yanked down, ripping off one of her nails. She put the bleeding ring finger in her mouth and a tear fell from her eye. Cold air pushed her underwear out from her body, tearing the fabric and ripping them off her. She scooted backward, hitting the couch with her shoulders. The cold wind played across her naked skin and tugged at the hooks of her bra.

"No. Please, Brian. Jacob. Whoever you are. Don't do this."

Fingers of ice grabbed her ankles and pulled her legs apart. A wall of cold pinned her upper body to the front of the couch, her hands to the floor by her sides.

"Please," she said.

The heart beat harder still, expanding to nearly twice its size and on contracting, jumped. *Tum-TUM* and every jump brought it closer to Bianca. Every time it landed, fluid squelched out of it and lay in stinking spots on the floor. Tears fell from her eyes and froze on her cheeks.

The stink of formaldehyde filled her nostrils as the heart got close. She could smell something else, too: an organic smell, like compost or meat that has been in the fridge two days too long. With it came that thick, cloying man-smell again.

The heart sprang forward, landing between her legs with a thud; some fluid squirted from an aorta, landing on her thigh. She screamed without sound.

The heart pushed up against her vulva, hot and slippery and pulsing. Her lips formed *no* over and over and she squeezed her eyes shut. She shook her head back and forth; it was the only part of her she could move.

The narrow apex of the heart nudged itself between her vulva, sliding up and down until it found the opening. The heart pushed inside her, thumping against the walls of her vagina with every beat.

Squeezing itself through in a reverse birth, the heart forced itself into her womb.

The cold released her and the fridge slammed closed. She fell to her side, gasping, sobbing and gripping her abdomen with both hands.

Inside, the heart beat against the walls of her uterus. Sudden, sharp cramps seized her; she yelped and contracted into a fetal position. When the cramping let up, she crawled to the bathroom. Lifting the toilet seat, she hung her head over the bowl. Guts lurching, she gagged. Spittle ran from her lower lip into the clear water. Tears ran down her face, mixing with snot and spit and dripping off her chin.

Levering herself up, one hand on the toilet bowl, the other pulling on the sink, she unbent her spine to look in the mirror. Her reflection's eyes went wide.

Bianca touched her fingertips to her all-white hair. Jaw slack, she moved them to her face, tracing the wrinkles and sunken cheeks. Curling back her lips revealed gums so dark red they were almost black and yellowed teeth a quarter inch longer than they were minutes before.

Dark brown spots spread across the backs of her hands and forearms. The bones in her arms stood prominent under loose skin. Her breasts sagged flat against her naked chest, nipples pointing to the floor. Lower still, her abdomen sank toward her spine and her hip bones jutted like wings. She could clearly see the outline of the heart beating behind her bellybutton.

Her legs gave out and she collapsed to the cold tile floor. The impact bruised her skin and dislocated her hip. The pain made her cry out; whimpers followed.

The door to her house opened, and she looked up without moving her head. Brown work boots, the tops obscured by faded blue jeans moved into view. Glancing up, she saw Jacob; she knew him, though he couldn't be more than twenty now.

The man squatted and picked up the empty jar and lid. His eyes met hers and he gave her a sad smile.

"Thank you," he said. "And, I'm sorry."

He stroked her hair with one hand. She closed her eyes and shuddered. Pulling a pocket knife from a pouch on his belt, he snapped out the blade. With a quick stroke, he opened a crescent wound in her abdomen, inches below her navel. she stiffened and hit him, but her blows had no strength. Wiping the blade on a hand towel, he folded it and put it away.

"Sh. Almost over now."

Reaching inside the cut, he pulled out the heart. He placed it in the jar. Blood pooling around her, Bianca watched. Her eyes blinked; the blinks got longer and she looked through a slight milky film.

Kneeling on the floor, away from the blood, Jacob unzipped his fly and pissed in the jar until it was almost full. The rank stink of formaldehyde stung her nostrils. He tightened the lid on the jar and gazed down at the old woman dying on the floor.

"I know this sounds crazy, but I kind of love you."

Bianca couldn't make her mouth work. With the last of her strength, she lifted one emaciated hand and gave him the finger. He grinned and nodded.

"That's the spirit. And, on the bright side, I won't have to have a garage sale for another fifty years. I hate garage sales; I really do."

Jacob carried his heart to the door with a spring in his step. He glanced back at the open bathroom door. As he watched, Bianca closed her eyes. She never opened them again.

Appetites

Curtis Wells was a foodie. Not a gourmet, no; it didn't have to be fancy to be good. He was a man who loved food of all kinds. This was evident by his prodigious belly.

Curtis was a large man, but he was fastidious, clean and well-groomed. He got expensive haircuts and wore tailored clothing. He spent a good deal of time in restaurants of all kinds, evaluating the food; he'd return to the good ones again and again. But, in his opinion, there was nothing like a home-cooked meal.

He was an accomplished cook, not chef caliber, perhaps, but he had a gift for knowing what spices to use, especially with meats. He enjoyed his own cooking, and enjoyed preparing food, but loved to eat at other people's houses. The combination of home-cooked food and the thrill of invitation made it special. This was particularly true the first time at someone's house, doubly so when it was someone nice to look at.

Michelle was decidedly in the latter category. Curtis had met her a few months back, at Firenze, an upscale Italian restaurant. She was his waitress three times in July, and they had a good rapport. Firenze had the best alfredo sauce Curtis had ever had; his favorite dish to order was shrimp with angel hair pasta smothered in alfredo. One evening, she brought it to him, and asked if he would like anything else.

"Yes," Curtis said. "I would like to buy you a drink sometime."

"I'd like that."

Later, when she brought the check, she put an extra mint on the tray; it sat on a folded piece of paper with her number.

He took Michelle to a nice bar not far from Firenze. They had drinks and talked, mostly about food, a passion they shared. He walked her to her car, where she gave him a friendly kiss on the cheek.

"I had fun," she said.

"Me, too."

"We should do this again sometime."

"Certainly," he said. "How about tomorrow?"

Michelle laughed. She got in her car, and looked up at him through the open door.

"Maybe Friday would be better," she said. "Call me?"

"Count on it," he said.

Michelle closed the door, gave him a little wave behind the glass and pulled away. Curtis watched her go. He was enjoying himself. The thrill of the chase appealed to him.

They went out that Friday, and the next. The sipped martinis in one place, microbrew beer in another; they always ordered the same dish, and it was always something new to them both.

One night, they sat in an Irish pub, drinking draught Guinness, surrounded by dark wood and serious drinkers, while overloud sea chanties played through the speakers. Michelle turned to him with a gleam in her eye. She leaned in close to yell over the music.

"I'd like to cook for you."

"Really?" Curtis leaned back to study her face. Michelle nodded.

"I'd like that very much," Curtis yelled back.

Michelle lived in a one-bedroom downtown. It was somewhere between affordable and pleasant. Curtis looked across the chocolate brown tablecloth, pale green napkins, unlit yellow tapers between him and the striking woman who had prepared their dinner.

She smiled at him and held up her fork, inviting him to use his own. Poised over his meal, Curtis relished the moment just before his first bite. The steam rose, brought the smell to him, teased him with hints of flavors to come. He took staccato sniffs, and let the air out all at once in a whuff.

Fork cradled in his plump fingers, he speared the first bite. Chicken on bowtie pasta with a creamy pesto sauce.

Exquisite.

Curtis finished eating, poured the few swallows of Shiraz down his throat and leaned back in his chair, hands resting on the swell above his belt. He belched, mouth closed, polite, and excused himself to his companion.

"Quite all right," she said. "In some cultures, that's considered a compliment to the chef." She smiled at him.

"Please consider it one. For this was a fine meal, and I am much impressed."

She nodded her thanks.

"My only tiny criticism would be that it could use a touch more garlic."

"You think so?" She asked.

"Oh, yes. In my opinion, you can't have too much garlic in this sort of dish. Garlic has many health benefits as well, and it keeps away mosquitoes."

"And vampires," she said. He grinned at her.

She set about clearing their plates and glasses. Curtis watched her, admiring the play of muscles under her tight green dress.

"How do you stay so fit," he asked. She looked back at him, bemused.

"Were you checking me out?"

"Yes," he admitted. "Your body is exceptional. It is a rare woman who appreciates food and remains so, ah, well proportioned."

"Thank you. I do triathlons. Five or six every year, and the rest of the time, I am training for one."

"I admire your dedication," he said. "I'm not much of an athlete, I'm afraid."

Michelle smiled and shook her head.

"I'm sure you have other things you're passionate about."

"Oh, I do," he said. "Things beside food, even."

"Perhaps later, you can tell me about them."

"Perhaps. Though I might like to get to know you better first."

"I'd like that very much," she said. Her voice was husky, full of promise.

"If I may be so bold, why would you be interested in me?"

"I like a man with healthy appetites," she said. "A man with some meat on his bones."

"Have you been with many large men?"

"Does it matter?" He shook his head. It didn't. Not at all.

She walked toward the hall, pausing to look back at him. He watched her, fascinated. Michelle pulled up the hem of her dress, reached under it and pulled down her yellow silk panties. She watched his eyes follow them as they fell to the floor. Stepping out of her underwear, Michelle went into her room. He was at the door in moments, hunger in his eyes. He held the discarded underwear on his right index finger; he twirled them around a few times, grinning like a kid, then let them sail across the room. She laughed and made a get-over-here gesture. Curtis was quick to obey. She threw off the covers and held a condom packet up, *ta-dah!* He took in her nakedness: smooth skin over strong muscles, a tattoo of a dolphin just below the navel, the hairless slit between her legs.

"You shave."

"Yeah."

"That's the sexiest thing I've ever seen," He said. She grinned at him.

She patted the bed next to her, and he lay down. She undid his pants and he helped her pull them off. Curtis peeled off his shirt as she tore open the package. He lay back and she rolled the condom over him. He watched her as she opened a bottle of massage oil and poured some in her hand. She stroked him for a moment, then slid her hand between her own legs.

"No foreplay?"

"I want to fuck," She said.

She ascended Mount Curtis, and slid him into her. Michelle held still, enjoying the moment, then gently rocked her body on his.

Curtis was gentle and attentive at first, trying to match her rhythm. Then, he was rough with raw need as he got close. Michelle almost climaxed with him, but he couldn't hold off long enough; it felt way too good.

"I'm sorry."

"Sh. Don't. Give me your hand." She showed him where to put his fingers and helped him move the way she liked. It only took a minute or so for her to come, too.

"Thank you." She rolled off of him, onto her back. She was breathing hard.

"Thank *you*," he said. "That was amazing." He ran a hand over her breast, index finger idly bouncing her nipple back and forth, back and forth.

"Careful. You get me riled up and I'll make you go again."

"Should I stop?"

"Absolutely not." She laughed. She had a good laugh that came from the gut. Curtis grabbed a Kleenex and stuffed the condom into it. He tossed both in the small garbage can by the bed. They didn't go again, but they played for an hour or so, exploring one another, content to touch and be touched.

He spent the night, and woke before Michelle. He gathered his things, showered and dressed and set about figuring out where everything was in Michelle's kitchen. In a low cupboard, he found a bag of good coffee. He filled the grinder to the top with shiny black beetle beans, wrapping the whole thing in a dishtowel to mute the noise. A few minutes later, the coffee maker beeped five times to let him know it was done. Michelle walked into the kitchen, wearing an extra large triathlon shirt, so old it was nearly transparent. Her hair was sticking up and out, comically cute.

"I slept in, huh?"

"I didn't want to bother you," he said. "You looked so peaceful."

"That's sweet."

"Coffee?" He gestured with the carafe.

"Please," she said. "I take it like my men, tan and bitter." He raised his eyebrows. She laughed.

"Just cream, no sugar."

"Ah," he said. "That's one I hadn't heard." He found half-and-half in the 'fridge, poured some into a *save the rainforests* mug and poured the coffee on top of the cream. When it was full, the cream turned it a dark tan. She took the mug in both hands, and sat at the table. He admired the considerable amount of thigh she revealed. His mind flashed to her naked groin. Such a lovely sight.

"Last night," he told her, "when you asked me in, I never thought I'd, ah, still be here in the morning."

"It's okay, though," she said, "right?"

"Much better than okay." He smiled at Michelle and toasted her with his coffee mug. His was an unadorned glossy black. It was the biggest one he could find. She toasted him back and they both sipped; it was still quite hot.

"I would like to return the favor sometime," he said, "and have you over to my house. I would love to cook for you. That is, if you, ah, want to."

"I'd be delighted," she said. "How about Friday? I have kind of a hectic week until then. Work has been a madhouse."

"Friday is perfect," he said. "That will give me time to prepare something really special."

"It's a date," she said. They shared an early lovers' smile, tentative and hopeful with a little naughty added in for spice.

Curtis took Friday off work to prepare. He had plenty of personal days built up; he was rarely sick and never went anywhere. He didn't enjoy travel; he didn't even like to drive, and did it as little as possible. He got up with the sun, and cleaned his house. He got out his best carving knife and sharpened it until it could cut a tomato effortlessly. He went to the farm stall just outside of town and bought fresh radishes, kale, and broccoli.

He dropped in to the bakery on the way home and bought a fresh baguette. Once home, he made a salad: vibrant greens, whites and reds. He made garlic bread with the baguette; he loved garlic, especially on fresh baguette. He put together a complicated marinade in a large bowl and set it in the 'fridge.

At five pm, he showered, and put on his favorite outfit, burgundy pants and a crisp white button-down, mild starch. He checked the clock: 5:50; he lit four tapers on the table and stood near the door.

The bell rang, and he checked his watch: 6:10. Fashionably late. He could feel his pulse in his temple. He waited a few seconds, forcing himself to breathe slowly, then walked four feet to open the door. Michelle wore a tan pant suit that might have been painted on. She grinned at him, hung her tiny purse on the coat hook by its spaghetti strap, and kissed him on the cheek.

"Hi."

"Hi."

"Smells good."

"Thank you. You look lovely."

"Not counting my shoes," she said, "guess how many articles of clothing I have on."

Curtis looked her over.

"Ah, three?"

"One." She gave a slow turn. Curtis noted the zipper that ran from the middle of her back all the way down, out of sight between her legs.

"That information," he said, "Is very distracting."

"Yeah," she said. "It's supposed to be. You going to give me the tour?"

He nodded, and showed her around his house. It was a modest, three bedroom ranch, but well-built and pleasant. There was a lot of natural wood and some exposed brick that gave it a country kind of feel.

He did not show her the basement. No other living soul had been in Curtis's basement since he moved in.

She proclaimed it cozy, and he had to agree that was a good word for it.

"Glass of wine?" he asked her.

"That would be lovely," she said. "White, if you've got it. I like the sweet ones."

"Certainly," he said. "Please, make yourself comfortable. I'll be right back." He gestured to the furniture in the living room.

Michelle sat on the loveseat. She thumbed through a book on Renoir paintings.

In a moment, Curtis returned with two glasses, one red, one white. He handed her the latter. She drank and made a face.

"Wow," she said. "This is *really* sweet! Did you add sugar?"

He frowned.

"No. It's from Portland; it's supposed to be good. I've never tried it before. Is it too much? I can dump it out and get something else."

"No," she said. "It's okay. I'll get used to it." She drank some more and smiled at him. He smiled back.

"So, what are we having? For dinner, I mean; I already know what I want for dessert." She waggled her eyebrows at him, a thing he'd never seen a woman do.

"Oh, it's kind of a specialty of mine," he said. "I've made it quite a lot, but it's different every time."

"I'm looking forward to it." Her speech was sloppy, as if she'd had four glasses of wine, instead of just a few sips.

"Oh, me too. Very much," he said. "I'm afraid, however, I'll be dining alone tonight, my dear."

"What? I don't understand." Michelle blinked away disorientation.

"Have some more wine, sweetheart. It will help clear your head."

She nodded and lifted the glass, sluggishly, but stopped herself. Her fingers lost their grip on the glass and it made a soft *bong* sound as it hit the thick carpet.

"You drugged me" she said. Her eyes glazed, and her head dipped forward as if she couldn't stay awake.

"It's okay. Don't worry. You're just fine. In fact, you're perfect. I have something to tell you, Michelle. Something you said the other day made me think of this, and I think it's pretty funny. Ready? I like my women like my coffee: ground up and in the freezer. Get it? I'm quite proud of that. I'm not usually funny."

Michelle said nothing. Instead, she lurched across the room, and hit Curtis in the face with her fist. It bloodied his nose and startled him. He fell back in his chair, which creaked in protest. In just a few seconds, Michelle was halfway to the front door.

Curtis moved fast, maneuvering his bulk down the hall, feet thump-thumping on the thin carpet. He caught Michelle as she was wrenching open the door.

He grabbed her about the waist and lifted her off the ground. She kicked out with both feet, closing the door with a bang and knocking him on his ass. He held on, but she wiggled out, adrenaline clearing her mind a bit and lending her strength.

She made for the door again. Michelle had her hand on the knob when lights exploded behind her eyes. Her knees buckled and she went down. Looking up, she saw Curtis, holding an umbrella by the fabric part. The wooden handle was broken, and, so was her head.

"Damn it, Michelle," he said. "Look what you made me do. Now, your head is no longer perfect. I am really, really disappointed in you."

"F-fuck you," Michelle managed, some fight still in her.

"No. We already did that. Now, it's time for our relationship to advance to the next level. It's time for you to become a part of me. Isn't that romantic?"

Michelle tried to hit him again, but her body betrayed her. The adrenaline was used up and the drug was pulling her down fast. She tried to spit in his face, but only succeeded in drooling on her chin. She raged against him, but it was internal. Her strong, athletic body was no longer hers to control.

Curtis lifted her off the floor and carried her to the kitchen. He laid her face down on the island with its thick, hardwood chopping block top. His thick fingers grasped the tiny zipper tab on her back after some fumbling, and he peeled off the pant suit. She was naked underneath, true to her word. He paused to pull off her high-heeled low boots, then pulled the clothes all the way off her. He pulled her legs apart, admiring the clean-shaven slit between her legs. It was somehow even sexier from this angle.

"Ah, Michelle," he said. "I can't get over how much I love your pussy. You know what? I think I'll keep it."

Bending close; he did the staccato sniff thing, inhaling the jasmine soap smell that enhanced rather than masked her own scent. He whuffed out the air in his lungs and planted a gentle kiss on her labia, then set her legs down.

He spun her around, her skin squeaking across the wood, and looked at her face. Her eyes were now closed, but he knew she could still hear him. The drug caused paralysis and a kind of torpor, but left the victim very much aware. Curtis had tried it on himself once, long ago, so he would know what to expect.

He rolled her onto her back. He stepped away for a moment, grabbed a red and white apron from a hook and put it on.

"This," he told her, "the first cut, is my favorite part. I'll never forget my first time; it was an accident really, a misunderstanding."

He pulled his carving knife from the block and slid the blade under her biceps, slicing through tendons and removing the meat from the bone. Blood fountained out, and made its way to the drain in the floor. He knew Michelle was screaming inside and he smiled at her.

"You're strong, my dear," he told her. "You'll, ah, last a while. So, anyway, that first time, I was just six years old. Little Katie Roberts, who lived next door was over, and we were playing doctor. Kids exploring, pretending at adulthood, you know? At first, I was the patient, and Katie examined me, looking in my ears, listening to me breathe. Then, on my turn, I wanted to play surgeon. I had seen, in a movie, doctors cutting people with blades, saving their lives. I took my father's hunting knife, very sharp and pulled up Katie's shirt. I cut into her abdomen, not very deep, but she screamed."

He leaned in close to her ear.

"I was thrilled," he continued, "but the grown-ups freaked out, so I knew something was wrong. The parents quickly convinced themselves it was a misunderstanding and my mother apologized to Katie's parents, explaining that I had seen surgery in a movie, and must have been emulating it. I understood, even then, that I needed to do more cutting. I also understood that I needed to be more careful, to not let on that I was doing it. Oh, Michelle, I'm ever so careful now."

He cut pieces from her and set them in a neat pile. At some point, the woman's heart gave out and she was still. He paused when he noticed. He wiped his hand on his apron, leaving a red smear, and stroked her hair.

"Thank you," he said. "For everything. I've really enjoyed spending time with you, and I'm sure you're going to make several fine meals."

After a couple hours, he had stripped most of the meat from her corpse. He looked at the skeleton: all bloody bones except for Michelle's face and cunt. He nodded. He had done well. With powerful hands, he wrenched the right leg off, then the left. He used his cleaver to sever the spine near the pelvis. Gently, he lifted the perfect, hairless pussy off the table and set it in the sink. He couldn't stand the idea of destroying it. He had never seen such perfection between a woman's legs. He would keep it, yes. How could he not? Yet, it was for display only, a small regret. He had so enjoyed sex with Michelle. That was all over now. He wasn't going to fuck the thing; that would be *sick.*

He rinsed off the blood, turning the pelvis over and around to clean it well. He set it down again and got back to work.

He trimmed the fat off the meat, and marinated it in the big bowl he got out of the fridge. He brought the cleaver down again, this time just under her head. He broke or chopped her bones into smaller pieces and loaded them into a vast pot, filling it with water and adding frozen beef stock. He started it simmering while he took her head and crotch downstairs. In the basement, he opened the padlock on the root cellar door.

He ducked under the low frame and stood up again in the small room. There were no roots here, no canned goods, no bottles of wine. The only feature in the room was a large steel door with a big handle and another padlock. It sparkled in the cool blue light of an overhead compact fluorescent in the ceiling. He unlocked this door, too, using a different key, and carefully placed the pieces of Michelle on a shelf, making sure they were not touching each other, or any of his other treasures. He stood in the cold room, admiring his trophies.

Annette, heavy on the oregano, pretty hands next to her head; Georgia, cinnamon and allspice, and her seven unicorn tattoos; Mary, thyme and basil, whose calves were shaped so nicely he had to keep them; Barbara, lemon grass and chives, and those perfect 36C breasts; and now Michelle, extra garlic and her spectacular cunt. He stayed, rapt with his treasures, until the cold ached in his bones and he had to leave.

Upstairs again, he cleaned up the mess, showered for the second time that day, and made himself dinner. It was sublime. The meat was done to perfection, though, if pressed, Curtis would have to admit that it was a tad gamey. After he ate, he wiped down every surface Michelle may have touched, wiped her cell phone's memory and shut it down. He put the purse, umbrella and her clothes in the incinerator. He would throw her cell into the river in a day or two.

He took her keys, drove her car back to her apartment, parking it in a legal spot. He cleaned off his prints, then went upstairs and obliterated every trace of himself from her apartment, too. While he worked, he breathed in the smells of Michelle and thought about the good times they had together. In the kitchen, he could smell stale coffee grounds; it sparked the memory of her coming out of her room in the big, threadbare t-shirt. He smiled. She was so cute with her hair sticking up all over. In the bedroom, he made sure she had taken out the trash with the condom in it. She had. When he was finished, he locked the door behind him, ending the chapter of Michelle's life with the click-thunk of tumblers.

Satisfied, he walked the four miles home; his back was soaked with sweat and his knees hurt, but he was happy. Michelle still had much to give him, and he would enjoy her for some time. He would eat well for the next few months. After that, he would have to hunt again. He was already thinking about what kinds of spices he might want to use next time.

Bed Bugs

Sean slapped his neck, killing another mosquito. He wiped the smear on his pants.

"This bug spray doesn't do shit."

Lara shrugged.

"They're not bothering me. You must taste better."

He leered.

"I've been told I taste pretty good, actually. Maybe you'd like to do a little research on that?"

She sneered.

"Not especially, no."

"Whatever." He slapped again, the back of his hand this time. "I thought you said it was a short walk. It's already been a long walk, and we're still not there."

She sighed.

"If I'd known you'd complain the whole time, I'd have left you at camp."

Under his breath, he said, "Bitch."

She faced him.

"That's right. I'm a bitch. And, bitches get shit done. If you want to walk your chicken-shit ass back to camp, go ahead. I'll be back by nightfall, and I'll take *all* the credit for anything I find. Do you understand me, Sean Gosen? You go back with nothing."

For a long time, he glared at her. She met his stare with flint in her eyes. He looked away first.

"Fine. Whatever. Can we just keep walking? The goddamn bugs are eating me alive."

Her answer was to spin away on a heel and resume hiking. Sean waved away the airborne mosquitoes in the air and followed.

It was another forty minutes before the orange marker appeared. Lara had hit a tree with a single burst from the spray can. She let out a relieved breath. It was easy to get lost in the jungle, but she'd found the spot without difficulty.

Above, the same conspiracy of lemurs played in the branches of the smaller trees. She recognized the markings of at least four of them. The one with the black ring around one eye, the one she had named "Pirate," stared at her, then at Sean, and back at her. He was holding a long, slithering millipede in his clever paws.

"Whoa," Sean said. "Do they eat those nasty centipedes?"

"Millipedes. And, no. They don't eat them. They do something far more interesting. Watch."

After the lemurs got used to the humans, they resumed darting around, searching for something. Pirate, who already found his, nipped the millipede, but not hard enough to kill it. The crunching sound made Sean wince.

"The millipede, when threatened, secretes a euphoric, hallucinogenic substance, which also acts as a powerful insect repellent."

Pirate rubbed the millipede on his fur, coating himself with the stuff. He kept nipping at it, making it secrete more of the toxin.

"That's messed up," Sean said.

"Nature is. Watch Pirate. He's the one with the patch up there. Watch his face."

Pirate stopped rubbing. He dropped the millipede, which seemed no worse for wear. Pirate's eyes half-closed; his expression totally blissed out.

"Ha! He's high as hell."

"Yeah," she said. "I think it's a narcotic, too."

"You think it'll work on humans?"

"Well, that's the billion-dollar question, isn't it? Can we isolate the hallucinogen, the narcotic, and the natural insect repellant from the millipedes excretions in a way that is safe and, it has to be said, profitable."

"You're so hot when you're greedy."

She reached out to shake his hand. With raised brows, he took her hand. She stepped in, pivoted, and threw him over her hip, so he landed hard on his back. The lemurs, at least the ones who were still sober, scattered.

"Ow."

"You will keep our conversations polite and professional from here on out, or I will break a bone next time."

"I believe you."

"Good. Get up. Help me catch some millipedes. Wear your gloves."

"Yes, ma'am."

The six they had managed to find rustled among dead leaves in a plastic tub with air holes in the lid. Lara hunched over a microscope, analyzing the excretions she had acquired by stressing the millipedes with a needle. Sean had soaked cotton balls from the bugs, and they had a decent supply.

He had been mostly silent since she threw him, and when he did speak, he was deferential. A mosquito landed on his bare calf; somehow, one had gotten into the tent. He squashed it with a palm.

"Damn it. The mosquitoes are killing me. Maybe these lemurs are onto something. I think I'm gonna put this stuff on me."

She didn't look up.

"I think that would be a bad idea. This secretion contains cyanide for one thing. Probably not enough to kill you, but I imagine it would make you uncomfortable."

"I'm already uncomfortable. And, if I get malaria, I'm going to be *seriously* uncomfortable."

Lara straightened. She stretched and cracked her back.

"Okay. I managed to isolate what I think is the narcotic. At least, the chemical that behaves like it is. How long have I been doing this? I'm half-starved."

Sean blinked

"Dunno. Half hour, maybe? Forty minutes? I'm kind of hungry, too, now you mention it."

"Okay. I'm going to go grab us both a meal. While I'm gone, I want you to harvest at least another half liter of excreta."

He sighed.

"All right. But, hurry, okay? And, could you grab a couple of canteens, too? I'm parched."

Lara nodded, pushed aside the netting at the tent flap, and left.

Sean poked and swabbed the millipedes, and poked and swabbed some more. He had about a third of a pint when a mosquito bit the back of his neck.

"*Fuck.*" He swatted it, and glared at the blood and mashed bug on his palm. The other hand held the cotton, wet with the millipede's defense mechanism. His gaze flicked from one hand to the other. He dabbed the stuff on the spot where he had been bitten.

It was cool and moist, but stung a bit on the site of the bite. He poked one of the arthropods with a needle, and soaked up the fluid, rubbing it on more of his neck.

Poke. Swab. Wipe. Repeat.

When all exposed skin was covered, Sean quickly revealed more. He stripped naked and dipped the cotton into the fluid he had collected earlier. He rubbed it all over.

Lara elbowed the netting aside, as her hands were full of food. Twin canteens hung from one shoulder. Once inside, she stopped cold.

Sean, nude and sporting an enormous erection, was drooling slightly and slowly stroking himself with one hand. His glazed eyes focused on her, and he grinned; it was somehow dopey and lustful all at once.

"What—" She saw the empty beaker and the cotton swab. Sean's skin glistened everywhere. She watched him work himself, entranced and repulsed. Her analytical brain, so good at noting details, couldn't help but see that he waxed, or shaved that part of himself. They'd been in the jungle for almost a week, but only a hint of a shadow showed on his skin.

He shivered and ejaculate spurted on his belly and chest. After a shuddering breath, he started stroking again. He didn't seem to be flagging at all.

"You put it on, didn't you?" She hunkered before him. "And this was the result.

"Fascinating."

She sat at the deck, snagged her notepad and wrote furiously. *This could be huge. The next Viagra. I'm going to be rich.*

She turned and came face-to-penis with Sean. It bobbed at the tip of her nose, gleaming with ejaculate. At first, she didn't react. Nothing in her experience had prepared her for this. She was about to threaten to sever it if he didn't move, when the smell hit her.

She knew it was the millipede excretion; she'd been working with it all day. But, it was mixed with the man's natural musk, and it was *different.* She was drawn to it, needed to get closer, to sniff, to touch, to taste.

She shook her head to clear it. She brought up a palm and banged the head of his prick with it. Sean jerked back, a pained look on his otherwise blissful face. He returned to his spot on the tent floor, where he picked up where he left off.

"Now, Sean," she said, "we can't anymore of that nonsense. Sneaking up on people with your, um, erection. We have to figure out why you're reacting this way, and see if we can duplicate it. I do believe our trip out here has just become substantially more lucrative. So, be a good boy now and stay there, while I get Smith and Jacoby. I'm sure they're going to be quite…impressed."

Her stomach growled.

"Right. First, I'm going to eat. You want yours now, too? Maybe you should wash your hands first."

Keeping him in sight, she ate the military-style ration pack. It was bland, but filling, and she washed it down with warm water from a canteen. He didn't eat; his hand never stopped moving.

"Don't go anywhere, big guy."

Dylan Smith and Becca Jacoby were a former couple who spent a year not working together after they split. They'd been back on Lara's team for almost six months now, and had maintained a mostly comfortable truce.

Sean kept trying to get *both* of them in the sack, preferably at the same time. If she had known how obnoxious he was going to be, she never would've allowed him to come along.

When all three women were in the tent, Dylan whistled.

"That thing's pretty big."

Becca hit her lightly.

"Almost makes you regret turning him down, huh?"

Dylan shook her head.

"Nope."

"No. Me either. How did he get like this? Not that it's much of a behavioral stretch for Sean."

Lara pointed at the millipede bin.

"He smeared himself all over with the excretions of these guys. The Black Lemurs use them to keep the bugs off. I imagine that was his goal, too. However, it seems to have had some interesting side-effects."

Dylan squatted a few feet from Sean. His head rolled toward her and he gave her a dopey smile. He pointed his penis in her direction, as if offering her some. She made a face.

"How long has he been, um, pleasuring himself?"

Lara shrugged.

"I left to come get you, and I wasn't here when he started, but I'd say at least twenty minutes. He's ejaculated at least once, with no sign of, er, flagging."

"Yep," Becca said, "if we play this right, we're going to be seriously rich."

"Did you observe this sort of behavior among the lemurs?" Dylan asked.

Lara shook her head.

"Not while I was there, anyway. It's possible that they became sexually charged after I'd left, but I doubt it; most of them seemed ready to pass out."

Dylan nodded.

"Okay. So, this is likely a side-effect specific to humans. How nice of Sean to discover this for us. Though, I have to say, he does seem pretty happy about it, too."

"I'm a bit worried about him, actually," Lara said, "despite how annoying he can be. The millipede excretion contains cyanide, as well as other chemicals I have yet to identify. These are undoubtedly flowing freely through his bloodstream by now, and may be causing irreparable harm."

Becca sniffed the air.

"What is that? It smells like," she turned to Dylan, "you. Sort of. It smells like sex, but nasty, too."

"Yeah," Dylan said. "I was thinking it, too, but didn't want to say anything. Do you smell it, Lara?"

"I do. I think it's the millipede stuff mixed with the sweat and sex smell coming from Sean. Earlier, it hit me pretty hard, and it was like the most powerful aphrodisiac. I was able to shrug it off, but I've noticed my body trying hard to react. I definitely have a wildly increased libido right now."

Becca slid a hand past her belt and between her legs.

"Jesus, I'm *wicked* wet."

Dylan's tongue ran across her top teeth.

"God, you're hot. I remember just how you taste, how I could make your toes curl, the feel of your fingers inside me."

Becca gasped as she worked herself, staring at Dylan.

"Um, guys? This is maybe not the time—" She stopped short. Sean's hands cupped her breasts; his erection pressed against her ass. The smell overwhelmed her and her logical, scientist's mind gave way to her lizard brain.

The three women hurriedly removed their clothes. Fingers, tongues and a single prick found their way into mouths and cunts. They became a sweating, writhing pile of limbs and erogenous zones.

The millipedes swarmed over one another in their bin. Their excitement mirroring that of the humans'.

When Lara woke, she was holding Sean's limp prick in her hand. Dylan spooned her from behind, one hand cupping one of her breasts. The tent reeked of sex, sweat and chemicals.

She slowly extricated herself from her sleeping, naked colleagues. She was sore inside and could taste one of the women on her tongue. She could only remember quick flashes of imagery from their small orgy, but it was enough to make her blush.

"Christ," she whispered. "This is powerful stuff."

Taking a long pull from the canteen, she looked around, trying to find her clothes. A groan behind her made her turn.

Sean was sitting up, covering himself with his hands.

"Oh shit. What happened? Did we just—" He blanched. "Am I fired?"

She laughed.

"Fired? Oh, Sean, no. You discovered something amazing, though profoundly disturbing in its raw form. Losing control like that was not acceptable. However, I am going to isolate whatever caused that...involuntary response and remove it. After that, my well-endowed friend, we, all of us, are going to be millionaires."

The other two were slowly waking up. They separated their clothing from Lara's and handed them to her. Sean's clothes were in a separate pile. They got dressed. Nobody spoke for a while. Finally, Becca cleared her throat.

"This stuff is dangerous, Lara. It's a date-rape drug waiting to happen."

Lara nodded.

"That had occurred to me, too. I'll need to isolate that aspect of it. I'm 85 percent sure I can create a formula that will increase libido and," she glanced at Sean, "stamina without the loss of control we just experienced."

"Jesus, I hope so," Dylan said. "Not that this wasn't a ton of fun, but I prefer to choose who to sleep with and when."

"Did I just fuck all three of you?"

Dylan laughed.

"Typical guy. No, Sean. We fucked *you.* And, each other. I think. It's a bit of a blur of body parts now."

For a while, they ate the food Lara had brought, and no one spoke. Sean snorted laughter suddenly.

"Stamina, huh? Awesome."

"Shut up, Sean."

Lara hovered over the microscope. Sweat trickled down her ribs, wetting her tank top. The heat had gotten unbearable the last few days, and she wore what she had slept in: the light shirt and underwear. Her hair was tied back, but hung damp and limp between her shoulder blades.

She leaned back and sighed. It was not working.

Reaching in to the bin, she caught a millipede and held it up. It curled around her fingers.

"Well, little guy, what's the secret, huh? How do we use your excreta to manufacture the next love potion? I know it's in there, because I *experienced* it. Help me out here."

The millipede wriggled in her hand. It stopped moving and was suddenly coated with the toxin.

"What? But, I didn't threaten you. I…"

She trailed off. The smell of the stuff was intoxicating. It smelled like ice cream, or candy. She brought her hand, and the millipede close to her face. She licked it, a tiny taste.

"Mmmm…"

Her tongue had pins and needles. Reaching into the bin, she pulled out the others, five in all. She set them on the floor, undressed and lay down next to them. She giggled.

"This is not very scientific."

She rubbed the millipede she still held on her breasts, her abdomen. She slid it under her arms, where the toxin mingled with her sweat. The scent of the two hit her sinuses and she was instantly wet between the legs.

"Oh god. Fuck science. I need this."

She brought the millipede to her mouth again. She licked along its length first, then took the front half into her mouth. The legs tickled her tongue as she slid it in and out.

The others crawled over her, adding their own excretions, mingling with her sweat. One nestled between her breasts; she squeezed them together around it with her arms. One found its way to her crotch and she gasped.

Pulling the first one out of her mouth, she looked down.

"Please. I want you inside me."

The millipede between her legs eased its way into her vagina. It released more of the toxin, and she had an immediate, mind-numbing orgasm. She resumed sucking on the first millipede, drinking the toxin filling herself.

She was on the verge of another orgasm when the tent flap opened. Sean stepped in and his jaw fell open.

She came violently, shuddering all over, squeezing the one inside her out onto the floor. Pulling the other one out of her mouth, she looked at him through hazy eyes.

"They seduced me. I needed to touch them, to feel them inside me. It's better than anything I've ever felt in my life."

She stood and moved to him. Peeling his shirt off his damp, sweaty chest, she ran her fingers through his hair. She undid his shorts and pulled them off, along with his underwear.

He watched her hands. His prick was already getting hard. She took it in her mouth, still tingling with millipede venom. She worked him for a while, then looked up at him.

"Lie down here."

He did, and she mounted him, taking in his considerable length an inch at a time.

The millipedes crawled over them both, writhing, excreting. She bucked on his, riding him hard and fast, and he tried to keep up. A millipede crawled under his balls and he gasped.

"Sh. Look at me. Watch me fuck you."

He obeyed, watching himself slide in and out of her. She fingered her clit furiously.

The millipede under Sean's balls crawled inside him, pushing its way past his sphincter and into his anus. He tried to tighten against it, pushing up and away, and driving himself deeper into her.

"Oh god, *yes*," she cried.

He bucked up, trying to get away, driving Lara crazy, but it just worked its way further in. The extra pressure made him ejaculate harder than he ever had, spurting into her over and over.

She screamed in pleasure as she rode out his orgasm with her own.

Finally, he stopped moving. She could feel him go limp inside her, and she slid off. Staggering on wobbly legs, she took a long pull from the canteen.

"I gotta tell you, Sean, I initially regretted bringing you along on this trip, but I think I may be changing my mind."

She laughed and glanced over her shoulder at him. He wasn't moving. He wasn't breathing.

"Shit. I killed him."

She dropped to her knees next to him, felt for a pulse at his throat. There wasn't one. She moved to start CPR, but she stopped. Something was very wrong.

Where are the millipedes?

Sean's abdomen moved. She jerked back, covering her mouth. She understood what has happening, but couldn't face it. Quickly, she pulled on her tank top and a pair of cotton shorts. She backed out of her tent, running to Dylan's. She burst in. Dylan and Becca were reading over reports, sitting together, each holding a different colored highlighter.

"What's up?"

"Sean. He's dead. I may have killed him. Or they did. Or both of us. I'm not sure."

Becca stood and took her by the shoulders.

"Whoa. Slow down. Sean's *dead?*"

Lara nodded. She left and went back to her tent, standing outside the closed flap. They caught up moments later. Dylan looked at her and pointed at the flap. Lara shook her head. She wanted nothing to do with it. Dylan pushed aside the tent flap and peeked inside.

She dropped it and threw up on Becca's legs.

"Shit!"

"Sorry. Omigod. Sorry. I didn't mean to. Don't go in there."

Lara stepped past them. She opened the flap. Behind her Becca said, "Jesus."

They were eating him. From the inside out, the millipedes were gobbling him up. It wasn't just the five she had been researching either. There were dozens of them.

She dropped the flap. Becca and Dylan looked ashen.

Lara was about to push them away from her tent, to insist they grab whatever gear and notes they can and run like hell. But she froze. She tingled all over, and she was so wet, it dripped down one thigh. Her breath came short.

"Oh my god, you guys," Dylan said, unconsciously stroking her thigh, "do you smell ice cream?"

Dead Set on Vengeance

Frank came home with empty pockets, sniffing and clearing his throat from too much coke. He had a black eye and his jacket was torn. He grinned at Valerie and grabbed her breast. Running his thumb over her nipple a few times, he licked cracked lips.

"Fix me a drink and get naked, babe," he said. He staggered into the bathroom and left the door open. Valerie did her best to ignore the sound of piss hitting water. She poured a shot of Amaretto into a short glass of milk. Checking over her shoulder, she pulled the brown glass bottle from the cupboard above the sink. She added a quarter teaspoon with an eyedropper to his drink and stirred it.

Frank left the bathroom without washing his hands. He had left the seat up again. She flashed him a brilliant smile as she handed him the drink.

"You're still dressed."

"Not for long, baby." She licked her lips. Frank knocked back the drink all at once, the way he always did. He frowned.

"What was that?"

"Amaretto in milk," she said. "It's supposed to be easy on the stomach when you've already partied a lot."

He set the glass on the counter hard.

"Well, don't give me that anymore. I don't like it."

"Don't worry. I won't." She walked toward the bedroom, rolling her hips. She looked at Frank over her shoulder, half-lidded eyes inviting him. He grinned and followed her. After three steps, he stopped. He put his hands on his stomach and his eyes got wide.

"What's the matter, Frank? Tummy ache?"

"What did you do?" He fell to his knees. He clutched his chest. His breath came rapid and ragged. Sweat beaded on his face.

"I poisoned you, Frank. It's potassium cyanide. It's no wonder you didn't like it." She squatted in front of him, just out of reach. Frank fell on his side, blinking constantly. His breathing sped up and his fist tightened, grabbing a handful of his shirt.

"Go f-fuck yourself."

She smiled.

"No. I'm going to go fuck *Phil*."

He glared at her and his lips moved soundlessly. His eyes bulged and his whole body shook. After a few seconds, he was still. She waited a full three minutes before checking him for a pulse. Not finding one, she washed her hands and pulled her phone out of her pocket.

"Hey. You remember how I asked if you could help me move some boxes? Tonight would be great, yeah. Thanks. See you soon." Hitting the 'end' button, she returned to the kitchen and fixed a cup of coffee. She spooned in a couple teaspoons of sugar. Frank didn't put sugar in his coffee; whenever he saw Valerie doing it, he'd tell her she was going to get fat.

"Yeah, well, you're dead now, so fuck you." Valerie toasted Frank's corpse with her sweet cup of joe. Setting down her mug, she went to the bedroom closet. After some digging, she came up with an Army green duffel. She laid it on the floor next to Frank's cooling body and went to the study. Dumping his papers from a few years back into two white file boxes, Valerie stacked them and tried to pick them both up, but could not. She carried them one at a time to the front door.

She drank coffee until Phil showed up. He stepped in, pushed the door closed with his foot and kissed her for a long time.

"Get the little bottle, honey. We need to dispose of it with the body." Phil unzipped the duffel and, starting with Frank's feet worked the corpse inside. In a moment, Valerie handed Phil the brown bottle with built-in eyedropper; he slid it into Frank's pants pocket. Soon enough, he was zipped up and ready to go. She grabbed a double handful of Phil's butt.

"Care for a quick tumble before we go?"

He grinned at her and shook his head.

"You want to screw around while your dead boyfriend is still in the house? You are one sick bitch, Valerie."

"Raincheck then."

Hefting the duffel to his shoulder, he carried it out to his pickup truck. With his free hand, Phil opened the back window of the cover and dropped the tailgate. He shoved the big green bag all the way back and locked the back of the truck. After another trip up and down the stairs, both file boxes were in the truck. They drove away.

Eighty minutes later, they pulled off the road onto a dirt track barely wide enough to allow the side-view mirrors. Sunlight, struggling to get through the overhanging foliage, flashed intermittently off the windshield. In a little over a mile, the dirt road widened and curved to the left. After a few bone-jarring potholes, they pulled up to a one-room cottage long past its prime. The front door was so warped the top leaned out a few inches; a thin film of dirt covered the front porch and steps.

Turning around in the yard, Phil backed the pick-up around the house. Keeping it under ten miles an hour, he navigated down the shallow decline to the wooden dock. He stopped and pulled the emergency brake before his back wheels hit the wooden boards. He and Valerie each carried a white file box to the canoe tied the end of the dock. Setting them in the boat, the lovers went back to the truck; they each took one end of the duffel and brought it to the canoe as well. Phil rowed them out the deepest part of the small lake. Unzipping the bag, he glanced in at Frank's pale, grinning face.

"He looks happy."

Valerie looked at her dead boyfriend and shook her head.

"He looks psychotic."

She opened the file box closest to her. Grabbing handfuls of papers, she shoved them into the duffel around the body. Across from her, Phil was doing the same. When all the paper was transferred, he zipped the duffel closed. It took both of them several tries to get the bag over the edge of the canoe. Twice, they almost tipped and went in, too. The duffel floated for a few seconds, causing Valerie's heart to pound, but then it slowly sank beneath the surface.

"Told you: wet paper is really heavy."

She nodded, still watching the dark green bag disappear. When it was no longer visible, she turned and grabbed Phil in a tight hug. They held each other for a long time. She finally broke the hug and grinned at him. He raised his eyebrows.

"What?"

"Why is American beer like sex in a canoe?"

"Because it's fucking close to water, of course," he said.

"Let's put that to the test, shall we?" She pulled her shirt over her head and unsnapped her bra.

"It's Miller time."

Four months later, they sat in her kitchen at the dinette table. On the fridge, there was still a picture of Frank and Valerie smiling on a Florida beach. Next to it was a missing-persons article cut out from the local paper.

Phil finished his beer; Valerie drained the wine from her own glass and stood up.

"Refill?" She looked at Phil; his eyes sparkled and a wicked smile curved his lips upward.

"I'm thinking we should move to the bedroom, actually," he said. She set down the glassware and reached for her lover's hand.

Half an hour later, drenched in sweat, she kissed him and stood up. He watched her naked body stretch and grinned. She smiled back and left him on the bed.

From the bathroom, Valerie heard a knock on the door. Finishing as fast as possible, she washed her hands and opened the bathroom door, still drying off. Holding the towel in front of her naked form, Valerie stood in the bathroom doorway. She flipped off the light behind her. Phil was on his way to the front door wearing only jeans. She watched, holding her breath. He glanced her way, saw the look on her face and gave her a thumbs-up with a reassuring smile.

Phil opened the door and his head jerked back, followed by the rest of him. Backpedaling away from the front door, he turned toward Valerie. His face was ashen, his eyes wide. His jaw worked but no sound came out. He put up a hand, palm out to Valerie and shook his head.

From behind the door, Frank staggered in. His skin was loose on his bones and pieces of it were missing. Frank had a single intact sheet of paper stuck to his chest; most of the ink was gone, but at the top in blue was 'W-2'. Valerie could see the outline of his ribcage through the tax form.

Stepping across the threshold, Frank kicked the door closed with his bare foot. His jaw dropped open and a wet hiss escaped. Phil recovered from his initial shock and charged him, fists up in a defensive posture. Phil had taken boxing classes at the Y a couple summers back. He threw a right hook at Frank, swiveling his hips and putting everything he had in it.

Frank made no move to defend against the punch and took it on the chin. With a jarring crack, his jaw came away from his head and bounced off the wall. Phil followed with a hard jab to the gut but hit him in the ribs instead. Phil hurt his left hand on the other man's bones and shook out his fingers, wincing.

Valerie dropped the towel and ran to the back door. She grabbed the baseball bat that leaned there.

Frank wrapped his own right hand around Phil's throat. Grabbing Frank's wrist with both his hands, he fought to pull it away. He couldn't budge the dead man's hand, so he went back to punching.

Frank moved forward, so he was inches away from Phil. Squeezing hard on his neck, Frank looked him in the eye. Phil couldn't get any punches to land hard this close, and his strength was fading as he ran out of air.

Bringing his knee up, Phil slammed hard into Frank's groin. The move had no impact on the other man; Frank brought his jawless head back a bit and slammed his forehead into the bridge of Phil's nose. All the fight went out of the other man; Phil went limp and blacked out. When there were two dead men in the room, Frank let him fall.

The second he did, Valerie swung. The smooth length of ash connected with Frank's head with a bone-cracking thud.

He turned his slightly concave face toward her; he lifted one hand and gave her the finger.

"You *shit*." She swung the bat again. She caught his elbow; with a wet crack, the arm snapped in half. The end hit the floor, middle finger still up. They both looked at it for a moment.

Lunging forward, Frank grabbed at her and only missed by half an inch. She stepped back and swung again, aiming for Frank's knee. The bat hit him in the thigh instead, but broke the femur, making him stumble and fall. Raising the bat high overhead, Valerie brought it down on his back, laying him flat. Bones broke with the blow. She lifted the bat for a second swing.

His good hand snaked out and caught her ankle. He yanked and she fell back hard on the floor. While trying to wiggle away from him, Valerie bumped into Phil. His purple face with bulging eyes sat above a throat with thin grooves cut into it from bony fingers. She shoved the body away from her and tried to swing the bat at Frank. It was impossible to get any real power behind it while lying down, but she managed to clip his head. It made a hollow *thunk*.

Pulling himself up by the grip on her ankle, Frank used his half arm on the floor for balance. He slid his body on top of her. She thrashed and battered him with both ends of the bat, held in the middle. The blows were making a mess of his face and one of his eyes ruptured; white fluid leaked onto her clavicle.

Positioning himself between Valerie's legs, he hovered over her, pinning the bat against her ribs with the weight of his upper body. He pushed his face onto hers, rubbing his upper jaw on her mouth in a mockery of a kiss. He lifted his pelvis a few inches up and brought it back down on her naked crotch. Panting breaths pushed out of his mouth, filling her nose with the stink of lake and decay.

She screamed at him and pushed, rolling her body to the side at the same time. She got him off her and scrambled to her feet. Before he could get up, she nailed him with the business end of the bat. This time, his head rocked to the side; neck bones snapped and flesh tore. He lifted his left hand and tried to put his head back where it belonged. She swung again, smashing that arm at the elbow.

The weakened limb fell off just like the first one. Frank stood, looking at her with his one good eye, head cocked at an impossible angle. Valerie, panting from exertion, peeled the wet W-2 form from her abdomen. She held the bat, resting the thick end on the floor. She lifted it a foot, looked at Frank, smiled and tapped the bat on the floor a couple times like she was waiting for the pitch.

Lifting it and bringing it to her shoulder, she paused.

"Go to Hell," she said and swung as hard as she could. The blow severed his head from his body; it hit the floor and rolled a few feet.

Dropping the bat, she staggered back to the wall. She slid to the floor and tears flowed down her face from behind closed lids. Shaking with shock and adrenalin, she took huge gulps of air between sobs.

Pain exploded in her side as Frank's headless body kicked her in the ribs. His eyes flew open. She dove for the bat. Her chest screamed in protest as she forced cracked ribs to move. She came up swinging, and this time nailed the knee on the first try. That leg snapped in half and the body fell to the floor.

Valerie brought the bat down again and again, smashing the bones of the legs and torso, the upper arms. Sweat dripped from her nose and chin; her hair was plastered to her head with it. From seven feet away, Frank's head watched her with his one good eye.

"You son of a bitch, why don't you die already?"

The skin crinkled around the severed head's eyes and the skin on the cheeks pulled up in the top half of what might have been a smile. She scowled and raised the bat to her shoulder. She took a step toward the head, but caught her foot on something.

Frank's hands were under Valerie; one was clinging to her left ankle and trying to climb her calf. The other hand was still giving her the finger. She kicked out with the leg with the hand on it, trying to dislodge the thing, but it held tighter and inched its way up.

Pushing at it with the end of the bat, Valerie tried to force the disembodied hand away; it clung to her, digging bonelike fingers into her skin. With a grunt, she took big, swinging strides to Frank's head, lifting the bat high once again. But, she only got one step before the other hand snagged her ankle and yanked. It hooked its elbow part against the door frame for leverage and she went down face first.

Pain shot through her head, from her nose outward. She lifted her chin, and blood flowed from her broken nose onto the hardwood floor. She flipped onto her back so she could use the bat.

Frank's left hand was holding both Valerie's ankles now, stretching its long, hard bone fingers to hold them in place. The right hand crawled insect-like up her thighs, dragging the stump along the skin of her legs. She swung the bat, but nailed her own thigh instead and cried out.

The hand reached toward her crotch, index finger and thumb clicking together like a claw. She shuddered all over and she dropped the bat. With both hands, she grabbed the hand, trying to wrench it off.

The hand clenched, digging in to her thigh. Two fingers broke the skin and went deep. The pain was incredible, but she pulled harder and got the hand away. When the fingers came free, blood fountained out of her leg.

That's the femoral, she thought.

Pulling hard with her abdominal muscles, she sat up. She grabbed the other severed hand off her ankles, taking some of her skin with it. She smashed both into the floor like drumsticks over and over until they were loose bones and pulp. They no longer moved.

Valerie was having trouble staying awake as her life flowed out of her thigh. She retrieved the bat though and crawled to where Frank's head lay. Kneeling, Valerie raised the bat and brought it down on what was left of him. Her cracked ribs protested; the movement forced more blood from her leg. She hit him again, putting everything she had into it. And again. And one more time. Finally, the light in his good eye went out. There was nothing left but the squashed skull on the floor.

"I win, you horrible fucker."

She fell to her side and wiggled over to Phil. On the way, Valerie snagged the towel off the floor. She held it against her wound, pushing down hard. With her free hand, she undid Phil's belt and pulled it off him in little jerks. When she had it tied around her leg, staunching the blood flow, she slid her naked body against Phil's. She sighed, shivered and patted Phil's pockets.

"Where's your phone, buddy? I'm pretty sure I need an ambulance."

Blackness crept in from the edges of her vision. She blinked it away and movement caught her eye. Something red, the size and rough shape of a slug was writhing toward her face.

"What the hell?" She could barely keep her eyes open, but between blinks, she watched the red slug. When it was inches away, she recognized it. It was Frank's tongue.

Valerie tried to back away from it, but Phil's body was in the way and she had no strength. The tongue pushed its way past her lips and into her mouth. Trying to bite down and spit it out at the same time, she fought as best she could, but the tongue persisted. It wriggled into her mouth, and tousled with her tongue for a moment. She gagged and gasped air through her nose; the drying blood inside made her breath whistle. Then, the last piece of Frank pushed its way into her throat, cutting off her air.

Lying naked on the floor of the front room, wrapped in a bloody towel, she choked to death on a dead man's tongue.

FuckKnot

Kerry stood, arms akimbo, on the tailgate of his Chevy Silverado and gazed out at his domain. That's what he was calling his quarter acre of woods. His "domain."

As inheritances went, it wasn't much. His late grandfather had sold off most of the land, parcel by parcel to get by over the last fifty-odd years. That included his house. This tiny bit, right off Rural Route 97, was all that was left.

When his wife had "disappeared," Kerry's grandfather moved into an apartment in town. Local gossip had it that the man had murdered his wife and buried her somewhere on his land. It was quite the scandal. Kerry found out about it when he was twelve.

He jumped to the dirt, flexing his knees on impact.

"Welp," he said to no one, "best get crackin'."

It didn't take long to explore the perimeter, marked by yellow ribbons every fourth tree. When he'd walked it, Kerry moved inward, diagonally from the southwest corner toward the northeast. Roughly halfway across, a huge oak dominated the other trees. It had to be as wide as his truck was long, and stretched hundreds of feet into the sky. Looking up at it was dizzying.

Kerry whistled. When his eyes dropped level again, they got wide.

"What the?"

Two fat branches spread before him. If he stepped up, he'd hit the crotch with his face. And, that's what it was: carved, or somehow naturally formed in the wood was a perfect replica of human vulva.

He laughed, looked around to see if there was a hidden camera, and scratched his head.

"I guess it's a cunt-tree." He nudged an imaginary sidekick. "Get it? *Country*?"

He checked his six once more, just to be sure no one was watching him, then tentatively put out a finger. The wood was as smooth as it looked and was warm to the touch.

He jerked his hand back. After a moment, he touched it again, caressing the folds. *Definitely warm*. He touched the tiny wooden clitoris and the tree shuddered. Leaves fell from on high.

"What the almighty fuck?"

Kerry took two steps back. He adjusted his pants, feeling a little silly getting hard because of a tree. He thought maybe Grandpa kept this one piece of land for a very good reason. He wondered if Grandma knew about it. Maybe they were into kinky shit together. He shuddered. Not the kind of thing you wanted to think about your grandparents.

Looking around once more, Kerry stepped back to the oak. He leaned in close, hands on either branch. When his nose was almost touching, he sniffed.

Yep, he thought. *It's faint, but it's pussy all right.* He put a finger to the lips, along the crack. Applying a little pressure, he slid it between the vulva. It went into the tree. He watched it disappear. His mouth hung open and his breath came faster. Inside, it was hot and wet, just like the real thing. He pulled it out. His finger glistened.

"Jesus."

He tasted his finger. It was tangy, sharp and a little nutty: *pecan, maybe?*

Spinning away from the tree, Kerry grabbed at his belt. He whipped his pants down and jacked off furiously.

It was over fast. He stood, panting, holding his deflating dick loosely in his left hand. After a moment, his pulse slowed. He snatched a handful of moss to wipe himself off.

"Whoa."

Kerry pulled up his pants and approached the tree. The pussy looked swollen, ready. He planted a gentle kiss on the wooden clitoral hood. "I'll be back."

Kerry parked his truck in front of the house. Billie got to park *her* car in the garage; it was nicer, newer, so it seemed fair enough to him. Certainly not worth arguing about anyway. Besides, his truck would take up so much room, he wouldn't be able to reach the lawnmower. It all worked out.

Opening the front door, he slung his keys on the peg over the mail slot. Reaching in, Kerry retrieved two bills, a credit card application, and a circular for the local dollar store. He would never shop there, but some folks did. Times were tight and you did what you had to. He tucked the bills under his arm and threw the rest in the square red bin by the garage door.

"Instant recycling," he said.

"Hey," Billie called from upstairs. "Izzat you?"

"Nope. Serial killer."

"Oh shit. Okay. Gimme a sec. I'll come down in my underwear and scream."

"Great. I'm gonna get a beer."

He did, and was drinking it when she appeared in the kitchen doorway. He frowned at her.

"You're not in your underwear."

"You're not a serial killer."

"Touché."

She kissed him on the corner of his mouth.

"So? What was it like?"

"Small. It was like a yard, only with all these … trees."

Billie cocked an eyebrow at him.

"Something happened."

He shook his head.

"No. I mean, yes, but no. Not really. It's silly."

"What? Was someone there? Is there some kind of legal dispute to your claim?"

He laughed lightly.

"No. No one was there. The land, such as it is, is mine. It was just weird, that's all. There was this one tree. It was, um, huge. And odd."

She took his empty beer bottle and set it on the counter. She pulled two more from the fridge, twisted off the caps and handed him one.

"Okay. Tell me about the big, weird tree."

He drank some. He looked Billie in the eye, looked away, looked back again.

"Shit, honey. I don't really know how to tell you. It was like nothing I'd ever seen before. You'll think I've lost my damn mind."

"I already think that."

He snorted once, a mock laugh. It was an old joke.

"Tell you what: in a week or so, I'll take you out there, and you can see for yourself. How's that?"

She drank some beer.

"I guess it'll have to do."

In the double bed that night, Billie turned off the light, rolled away from him and spooned her back against him. In the dark, Kerry pictured the tree. He felt its warm, wooden cunt, smelled the musky pussy scent. He got hard and pressed himself against Billie's buttocks.

Her breath caught and she pushed back. Kerry pulled up her nightshirt, then hooked her underwear with a finger, sliding it to one side.

"Mmm," she muttered.

He eased a finger along her vulva, softer than the tree, warmer, too. He found her clit, tickling and twitching it. Billie rocked her pelvis a little, encouraging him. She was already wet, and he slid a finger inside. Hotter, but not as tight as the tree.

With his eyes closed, Kerry pictured the tree. Saw its welcoming branches, smelled its nutty cunt. He withdrew his finger, replacing it with his cock. Mentally fucking the tree; actually fucking his wife. Side by side, they rocked faster and faster. Their breath came shorter. Their hearts pounded.

They came.

After almost a full minute, Billie caught her breath enough to speak.

"H-holy shit."

Grinning, Kerry nodded.

"Yeah. That was awesome."

The next day, Kerry drove to what passed for downtown in their sleepy little town. Nelson's diner (with the badly painted, faded, copyright-violating yellow-skinned cartoon character painted on the window, sneering, pointing and saying "Haha" in a word balloon.); Barnes' Hardware; Smokey's Tavern and the Brookfield General Store. The latter was run by Fred Winston, who was something like a hundred and forty years old.

Kerry stocked up on canned goods, five pound bags of flour and rice, and a couple cases of PBR.

The oxygen tank puffed into Fred's nostrils as he checked off Kerry's groceries at a glacial pace. Kerry paid him.

"See you next time, Fred."

"If I (puff) live that long."

Same shit, different month.

On the way home, listening to one of nine country stations his radio picked up, Kerry saw the sign for Rural Route 97 and his balls tingled. He glanced in the rearview. He had the road to himself. *Who's gonna know?* At the intersection, he veered right and headed toward his new property. His "cuntree."

By the time he crossed the yellow ribbon threshold, Kerry was hard. For a long time, he stood, motionless, in front of the tree, gazing at the wooden pussy.

"Um. So. Hi, I guess. I don't know if you can hear me, or understand me, but I can't get you out of my head. I think about you all the time, even woke up with a hard-on from dreams about you."

The tree didn't move, but Kerry could smell the vagina now. The lips swelled a little, maybe. It was hard to tell.

"So, um, I'm gonna, well - how to put this delicately - I'm gonna go down on you now. I hope that's cool."

He looked around. Except for a spring peeper somewhere, he was alone in the woods. Kerry wrapped his right arm around a branch and put his face in the crotch. His left hand stroked himself as he ate the tree out.

Thick, sweet sap leaked into his mouth. He swallowed it. He flicked his tongue around the tree's clit, dancing it up and down, side-to-side. With his palm, he used the wetness oozing from his prick to lube himself and pumped harder.

The tree pussy was hot against his face, the lips yielding to his. More of the sweet sap slid in his mouth, the taste filling his head; it was intoxicating. He shuddered, spewing spunk on the trunk. At that exact moment, the whole tree shook against him and leaves rained on his head.

Kerry laughed. He staggered back and pulled up his pants.

"Whoa. That was nuts. Great, but nuts. Heh. No pun intended there. Seems like you enjoyed yourself, too. Hope so. I'll be back. Oh yeah. I'll be back." He stroked her limb on what would be a woman's upper, inner thigh. "And, next time? I'll bring a ladder."

When he got home, Kerry put six beers in the fridge and the dried goods in the pantry. Eight built-in shelves recessed into one of the kitchen walls. But, Billie liked to call it "the pantry" so that's what it was.

She came in from the garden, with filthy hands and dirt on the knees of her jeans. She kept her hands wide and gave him a quick kiss on the lips. She made a face.

"You smell funny."

Kerry turned away to hide the blush.

"I need a shower. Forgot to take one this morning."

"Ew. Gross. Go ahead. I'm after you."

Later, as they were getting ready for bed, Kerry sized up his wife. She caught him at it and, wearing only her underwear, tilted her head to the side.

"What are you contemplating?"

"Um, would you mind, uh, getting on the dresser?"

She stared at him.

"On *top* of the dresser?"

Kerry nodded.

"Naked. Please."

She cocked her head. A smirk tugged at her lip.

"This is some kinky shit, boyo."

"I know. Humor me?"

Smiling, Billie shook her head. Wiggling her hips, she eased her underwear down until gravity took it. For a moment, she looked at the dresser, then looked around.

"Hang on," Kerry said. From the closet, he pulled a step ladder that folded out to four feet tall.

"I thought that was in the garage."

Kerry blushed.

"It was. I, um, moved it."

"You *planned* this little adventure?"

He nodded.

"You sick little monkey."

Climbing slowly, looking over her shoulder to make sure he was watching, Billie eased herself onto the dresser. She sat facing him, legs slightly apart.

Kerry leaned on the ladder and for the second time that day, buried his face in a crotch. He worked her with his tongue until she was squirming, gasping. He stopped.

"Aw."

"Wait a sec," Kerry said. He pulled off his own underwear. His cock popped out and bounced. It was comical, but he stifled the laugh. He didn't want to kill the mood.

Mounting the ladder, he positioned himself carefully and slid inside her. She was already wet and hot. She groaned in pleasure as he sank to the hilt, and put her hands on his shoulders, pulling him to her.

She matched his rhythm as best she could from the awkward height and angle. Despite the fact that he'd already had three orgasms in two days, Kerry exploded into her very quickly.

She wasn't done, though, so she hooked her legs behind him, forcing him to stay inside her and finished herself off with her fingers.

They almost fell twice.

When it was over, he climbed down, followed by her. They got cleaned up, into pajamas and laid on the bed. The ladder was still in front of the dresser.

They both looked at it.

Billie turned to him.

"Well, that was different."

"Uh huh."

"Fun, though."

"Yeah."

She kissed his cheek.

"'Night."

"G'nite. Love you."

"I love you, too, you big weirdo."

She was smiling, though.

He went back to the tree the next day. He hauled the ladder out of the trunk and carried it under one arm.

When he opened it before the tree, he wagged his eyebrows.

"Told you. Now I can reach."

He glanced around, but no one was there. Kerry peeled off his shirt and then took off his pants. He left his boots on because he was outside and outside, you wore boots.

As he did with Billie, Kerry leaned forward on the ladder. He licked along the crack of the vulva, easing them open with his tongue. It was already warm and wet.

"You've been expecting me."

He slid two fingers inside. They disappeared into the wooden folds. He watched them slide in and out, fascinated.

"Okay. Are you ready?" He glanced down at his erection. "I know I am."

Stepping up, one foot at a time, prick bobbing its head, Kerry positioned himself before the tree. With one last furtive glance behind him, he pushed his way in.

The tree's cunt squeezed gently. He gasped at the sudden, intense pleasure of the pressure. Gripping fistfuls of bark, he pulled back and slammed it home again.

"Omifucking*God*. This feels good."

He fucked the tree slowly for as long as he could stand it. Then, he picked up the pace, pounding himself inside over and over. When he felt the pressure build in his balls, he pushed himself all the way in.

The tree squeezed him hard, just like a real woman does when she comes. The inside pulsed around him, milking his cock. He shot into the wooden cunt again and again.

Finally, spent, he relaxed. The tree let go and he slid out with a faint "pop."

Kerry leaned his forehead on the trunk. The rough bark was cool on his skin. He caught his breath enough to speak.

"Wow. That's all I got. Just … Wow."

"Do you believe in fairies?"

Billie turned toward him. The plate in her hand dripped suds on the floor.

"What? Like Tinkerbell?"

Kerry scoffed.

"No. Like, I don't know, tree spirits and shit."

She finished washing the plate and rinsed it, setting it in the drainer by the sink.

"Where are you going with this?"

He shrugged. She rinsed her hands, dried them thoroughly and put her hands on her hips.

"Listen, mister: something's going on with you lately. I haven't said anything, because apparently whatever it is making you crazy horny and experimental and I've been enjoying that. But, you come home smelling funky - almost like another woman, but not enough to make me suspect you're cheating. And now, you're asking me about fucking fairies? What the hell, Kerry?"

He took a long pull off his beer, avoiding her eyes. When he finally looked, she was clearly pissed. He sighed.

"Honey. I don't know how to tell you this…"

"Spit it out."

"You know that land I got from my grandfather?"

"Yeah."

"Well, after my grandma disappeared … did I tell you people thought he killed her?" She nodded. "Thought so. Anyway, once she was gone, he moved into town and sold it off, parcel by parcel. Except for this one tiny part. That's what he left me."

"Yeah. Get to the point."

"I'm working on it. Okay. This tiny parcel. There's this tree there. It's, um, it has a … pussy." This last was almost a question.

"What?"

He laughed weakly.

"I know how it sounds. Crazy, right? But, it's true. It's a real, honest to god, human pussy made of wood."

She stared at him for so long, he had to look away. He tried to drink from his beer can, but it was empty. Finally, he looked at Billie again. She shook her head.

"I want to see it."

"I don't know if-"

"I want to see the 'tree pussy' you've been fucking. You have been fucking it, haven't you?"

His face got hot. He looked away and nodded.

"You cheated on me."

"It's a *tree*, Billie."

"Did you enjoy it? Did you come?"

His answer was barely audible.

"Yes."

"I'm pretty sure that's still infidelity, even if it's with a fucking plant, man. Take me there. Now."

The Silverado rumbled up Rural Route 97. The radio was silent, and so were they. Kerry pulled over, yanked up the e-brake and killed the engine. He looked at Billie; she turned from the window and met his eyes.

"I'm sorry, okay? I should have told you."

"Yup."

"It just kind of happened, you know? The whole thing was crazy and weird, and I got carried away, I guess."

"This has to be the worst apology ever."

Kerry chuckled.

"Yeah. It sucks, huh?"

She got out of the truck and he followed suit.

"Okay. Let's go. I wanna meet the hussy who's been with my man."

"You're so weird sometimes, honey."

"I'm not the one having carnal relations with an oak tree."

"Good point."

Their feet swept through a blanket of crunchy leaves, mostly brown, but with some red and yellow mixed in. Kerry led her around the tree to the other side, the side with the cunt.

For a long time, Billie looked at it.

"Huh. Looks just like the real thing, doesn't it?"

"Yeah. Feels like it, too."

"*Dude.*"

"Sorry. That was tacky. But, I mean, see for yourself. Touch it."

"I'm not really into girls."

Kerry sighed.

"I know. I've always kind of been sad about that."

She laughed.

Reaching a tentative hand out, Billie touched the outer edge of the tree's vulva. She pushed on it with her fingertip, forming a slight depression in the wood. When she pulled away, the dimple slowly filled in again until it was smooth.

"Whoa."

Kerry hugged her from behind. He pushed his erection against her ass. She tensed, but didn't pull away. After a moment, she relaxed and let him hold her.

He kissed her ear gently and whispered.

"Taste it."

"What? No."

"It's like syrup, kind of. I don't really have the right word. Go on. I won't tell anyone."

Billie pushed her finger between the pussy lips and watched it slide inside.

"This is the most fucked-up thing I have ever done."

Kerry fondled her breasts through her shirt. Her nipples hardened immediately. He was breathing hard.

"It's so hot, though. I'm so insanely horny right now."

"Yeah. Me, too."

"Come on. Taste it. Put your finger in your mouth."

Billie pulled her finger out of the tree, wet and shiny. She turned it, looking at it. Finally, she touched the tip to her tongue. After a moment, she slid the whole digit in her mouth.

"Mmm. Sweet."

Leaning forward, Kerry turned her head by her chin. He kissed her deeply, tasting the cuntsap in her mouth. He fumbled at her belt. She put a hand on his.

"Wait. This is crazy."

"Are you wet?"

"Yes."

"Show me."

Billie undid her belt, her jeans, and led his hand inside. He slid a finger in her, eliciting a gasp.

With his other hand, he pulled his own pants down. She reached back and stroked him.

"I have a totally sick idea," she said.

He grinned, fucking her hand.

"What?"

She dropped to her knees and took him in her mouth. She sucked him for a moment, then looked up and met his eyes.

"I want to watch you fuck the tree."

"Really?"

Billie nodded.

"Every time you get it on with this thing, you come back and rock my world. Besides, it's not like I can be jealous. I mean, it's a *tree* for fuck's sake. Also, this is the closest you're ever gonna get to an actual threesome. You should take it."

Kerry jerked his pants up. She glared at him.

"What the hell?"

"No. I want to. Hang on. I have to get the ladder out of the truck."

She laughed.

"Don't take too long."

"Not a chance."

Even though running with a hard-on was awkward, he was back fast. He started to climb, but Billie put a hand on his arm.

"Me first."

She kicked off her pants and climbed the ladder half naked. Levering up on a branch, she positioned herself so her crotch was right in front of Kerry's face when he was on the ladder.

"In case you feel like a snack."

He licked his lips and waggled his brows. Running the tip of his prick along the crack of the tree's cunt, he found the sweet spot and slid in. The "muscles" inside gripped him, making him shudder.

Billie slid closer so he could reach and he dove in, licking and sucking. It was incredible to be giving his wife pleasure this way and getting laid at the same time. He slid faster in and out of the tree. Billie, holding herself up with one hand, put the other on the back of Kerry's head. She was on the verge, and he wasn't far behind her.

She climaxed and damn near fell out of the tree, scrambling for a handhold.

He came, too, thrusting as deep as he could into the tree's hole. The pull from within was intense, painfully so. He pulled back, but was stuck. His face must have shown his panic.

"What? What's wrong?" Billie asked.

"I don't-"

He screamed.

Kerry fell away from the tree. Blood fountained from the hole in his body where his dick used to be.

The lips of the tree-cunt were squeezed together tightly, blood spattered the edges, a Rorschach blot in red.

The ladder toppled sideways.

Billie scrambled to the ground, scraping her bare legs and ass on the bark.

She grabbed his jeans, bunching the fabric, trying to staunch the blood flow.

"Kerry! Honey, don't die. Oh my god, oh shit, oh fucking Christ."

The denim grew dark and wet in her hands. His face paled. His eyelids fluttered. His voice was a squeak.

"I'm - I'm sorry. This was a bad idea."

"No. Shh. This was my idea. You just relax. I'll call 911. You're gonna be okay."

He shook his head, or tried to.

"I don't think so."

Billie reached behind her, feeling around for her pants. The phone was in a pocket. Finally, she found them and dragged them over. Furiously, she scrambled to get the phone out with one hand and to hit the button for emergency. The blood on her fingers made it really hard to swipe the screen.

Kerry coughed. Weakly, he tapped her leg.

Focused on the phone, she didn't look.

"What?"

He pointed.

"Tree."

Billie stopped trying to get the screen to clear and turned her head.

Blood ran in a line from the cunt. It looked like it was menstruating. Halfway to the ground from the hole, the blood ran on either side of something that had not been there before.

A cock. It looked exactly like Kerry's, only wood, and poked out, hard as hell, from the trunk.

"That's your dick," she whispered.

"Uh huh."

"This is a nightmare."

"Look on the bright side," Kerry said. Blood trickled from the corner of his mouth. He coughed, chest spasming. "When I'm dead, you can still come out here and fuck me."

"Dude, that's sick."

He barked a short, wheezing laugh.

"You know what's worse?"

"What?"

"My grandpa's wife supposedly disappeared in her thirties. Maybe she was here the whole time, in the tree. I could have been fucking Grandma Simmons' pussy."

"Yeah. That's worse, all right. Jesus, honey. You don't look good."

"Sorry. I love you, though. That should count for something."

She stroked his hair. Her bloody phone sat on the ground forgotten.

"It counts for a lot. I love you, too."

"Billie?"

"Yeah?"

He tried to tell her to soldier on when he was gone. That he was sorry for bringing her here. That he never should have touched the damn tree. But, he couldn't make his mouth work. He looked at her face, beautiful despite swollen eyes and dirty tear streaks. He reached out a hand to touch her, but she seemed so far away.

He blinked. A warm, yellow light filled his vision. *That's nice*, he thought. It faded slowly, along with the pain in his groin. He closed his eyes and was gone.

Stiffed
(with Kerry Lipp)

Jason rolled away from his wife. Callie was like a radiator. He threw the blanket off, then the sheet. *Better.* He tried to get back to sleep, but couldn't. He stood and pulled on his old flannel robe. The floorboards were warm under his bare feet, and he was glad he had fired up the furnace. It was lovely this time of year, with the changing colors and bright blue skies, but it got cold at night. It seemed extra cold now.

Jason moved through the quiet house, not turning on any lights; he could see well enough to avoid the giant toy truck his son had left on the floor. He used to push Cal around in the back, but now the boy towered over it. Even at ten, Cal still played with it. His son flat-out refused to let his parents get rid of it.

He considered making coffee, but didn't want to run the grinder and wake the others. Besides, he didn't want any, which was crazy. He always wanted coffee.

Instead, he poured himself a half glass of orange juice. Jason sat down at the kitchen table and held the glass turning it one way, then the other. It looked strange, alien. Which was weird. He had been drinking OJ for thirty years.

He stuck his finger in the juice and licked it. It tasted like nothing. He did it again with the same result. He decided not to drink it after all. He carefully poured it back in the carton (in case it was just him and not the juice) and rinsed the glass. He shook his head. *Maybe I'm coming down with something.*

Jason shuffled to the bathroom; his feet felt like wet clay. He pulled the door shut before turning on the light. He looked at his reflection: pale, with slightly sunken eyes and cheeks. He leaned in close to look at his eyes. They had a filmy, glossy look he didn't like. After a while, he noticed something was missing.

The mirror wasn't fogging up. He put his hand before his mouth and tried breathing on it. He couldn't seem to push air from his lungs. It was the strangest thing. Almost as if he had forgotten how to do it.

He was still standing there fifteen minutes later when Cal knocked on the door, startling his father.

"Dad? Are you almost done? I have to pee."

He pushed himself away from the sink. His back, neck, arms and legs were stiff and hard to move. With a numb hand, he turned the knob. Cal looked at him and the boy's eyebrows crawled up.

"What?"

"You don't look good. You should stay home today."

"Maybe you're right," Jason said, thinking about the orange juice and the lack of fog on the mirror, not to mention the reflection that stared back at him.

Cal brushed past his father in the doorway and paused, looked his father up and down, sniffing.

"And, Dad. Don't take this the wrong way, but you … well, you kind of stink."

Before he could respond, Cal closed the door and Jason could hear the rush of urine hitting the toilet water.

I stink? He sniffed under both arms, but didn't smell anything. Then he thought maybe it was his breath. He held a hand in front of his face and blew into it. Again, he felt nothing as he exhaled. Nor could he smell his breath.

Maybe the boy was just messing with him or maybe this was all just a weird dream degenerating into nightmare.

One more test, he decided and then he'd go back to bed and start over when he woke up.

He went back into the kitchen and grabbed a bottle of air freshener from under the sink. He hated these things, always trying to mask something worse and instead creating something even more stomach churning.

He figured he'd be able to smell it, and if he really did stink, he could spray a little on himself so Callie wouldn't be repulsed when he made his way back to bed.

He read the can: it claimed to be refreshing vanilla with a hint of lavender. He pulled the trigger and walked into the spray.

As he feared, he smelled nothing. This whole morning was beginning to freak him out. He still didn't believe it. People didn't just wake up without a sense of taste or smell. This had to be a dream.

Since he was dreaming, Jason turned the nozzle straight to his face and squeezed the trigger. He heard the sizzle of the spray escaping, saw the mist shoot directly into his eyes, nose and mouth but smelled nothing, tasted nothing, and felt no wetness on his face.

He wanted to scream, but he didn't want to scare his son. Not that it would wake Callie up. She slept like a rock. And if he did wake her up, he knew how chipper she'd be. Hell, grumpy Callie had made him *wish* he was dead more than once.

He tiptoed back to the bedroom; he could hear the shower running behind the bathroom door. He saw the steam leaking from underneath, and as it touched his ankles he couldn't feel the heat. He could no longer feel the warmth from the floorboards either.

The lack of sensation was hard to describe. The floor was just solid. That was it, like walking on a foot that had fallen asleep without the prickle of pins and needles.

So weird, he thought as he slipped back into the bedroom. Callie lay on her side with her back to him; he took off his robe. Jason gazed at the curve of his wife's hip. He may not like her much as a person, but he'd always found her sexy, especially when she was lying on her side. He stared, but nothing stirred in his pajamas. Slipping beneath the sheets, he felt no heat nor chill either. He didn't feel the fabric on his skin.

He rolled onto his back and heard something wet squish beneath him. He sat up, threw the covers back and saw why Cal had said that he stunk. Matted and smeared into the sheets on his side of the bed was a lump of brown shit.

It had to be his, but he had no recollection of shitting in the bed.

Just what the hell was going on?

This—shit— on top of all the weird events of the morning was too much. He let loose a piercing scream. Long enough and loud enough to wake Callie who rolled over and looked at him.

"Jesus *Christ*. What the hell, Jason?"He tumbled out of bed trying to get away from the shit, from his wife, from this whole day. Callie looked at the stinking brown smear on the bed that led to her husband. Her look of disgust hit Jason like a slap in the face."I don't think I can ever let you touch me again. And, I am *not* cleaning that up."

She launched herself out of bed on her side, shuddered once, and left him standing there, confused and angry and hurt. He had been cowed by his wife for years, but he was having a rough morning; she didn't have to make it worse. He stripped the bed, careful to contain the mess, then stripped himself. He wiped his body with the clean parts of the top sheet and put everything in the hamper, thankful he had lost his sense of smell. He stood naked in his room until he heard the bathroom door open and his son's bare feet padding down the hall. Holding a clean towel in front of him, Jason slipped into the bathroom and showered.The water must have been hot, as there was steam everywhere, but he couldn't feel it. He got clean, got out, and wrapped the towel around his waist. He wiped off the mirror and watched as his red skin turned white. It didn't take long. *I still look like hell, but at least I don't stink.* At least, he hoped not. His nose still wasn't working.He got dressed in his room. The mattress was still exposed. He considered making the bed, but it seemed like too much work. It was weird, not being able to feel the clothes as he pulled them over his skin. On an impulse, he pushed his fingers into the hollow of his left wrist, looking for a pulse. Either there wasn't one, or his numb fingers couldn't find it.Jason walked through the house; he stood in the kitchen doorway for a moment, watching Callie and Cal. *I wanted to name him Robert*, he thought for the billionth time. Finally, his son noticed him."Hey, Dad." His son spoke around a mouthful of toast. Jason gave the boy a little wave."I think something may be very wrong with me," he said to Callie. "I might be really sick."

She gave him a look that failed to contain any sympathy."Call Bob. See if he's free."

Bob was one of his oldest friends. He was a podiatrist who used to be a general practitioner; he specialized a few years back for the money. He was a good guy, and he'd do house calls for Jason and his family.He showed up ninety minutes later with his stethoscope, reflex hammer and that thing with the light for looking in ears and noses. *Otoscope*, Jason remembered. Bob examined him. Then, he shook his head and ran the test a second time."I got some bad news for you, bud. You're dead."

Jason was sure he had heard that wrong.

"What?"

"I took your vitals, man. You don't have any. Also, for some reason you smell kind of like vanilla.

Jason shook his head, not comprehending.

"I can't smell anything. Why the hell would I smell like vanilla any—" Jason broke off and remembered the air freshener. It must not have washed off in the shower. He remembered the lack of pain or sensation that accompanied it. He thought about not being able to feel his clothes on his skin and the taps from Bob's reflex hammer that he barely reacted to.

"Oh shit."

What was happening?

"Christ, you look like you just saw a ghost," Bob said.

He grabbed Bob by the collar and pulled him close. Their faces were inches apart and his eyes flicked from his friend's right eye to his left and back. And again.

Several times. After a moment, Jason released him.

"I'm sorry. I'm scared. I can't feel anything. I can't smell anything. I can't taste anything. I shit the bed this morning. You tell me I've got no vitals and I look like hell. I can't be dead, Bob. Look." He moved his arms around and did a little dance in front of Bob.

Bob stared at him.

"And my brain works too, Bob. Just fine. Ask me anything."

"What day is it?" Bob asked.

"Thursday."

"What's your full name?"

"Jason Alexander Harding."

"What was my nickname in college?" Bob asked.

"Goblin," Jason shot back.

"Why?"

"The way you ate. You gobbled everything like someone was about to snatch the plate away."

"What day is it?"

"Thursday," Jason said. "You already asked me that. You got a scalpel in that bag?"

"What?"

"A scalpel."

"Uh… Maybe…" Bob nodded.

"Good." Jason rolled up his sleeve. He presented his arm to Bob.

"What are you doing?"

"Cut me. I want to see what happens. Maybe that'll provide a clue."

"I can't just cut you."

"Fine, I'll get a knife and do it myself." Jason stood and turned toward the kitchen.

"Sit down, you stubborn asshole." Bob pulled a scalpel from his bag. "Where do you want it?"

"Just nick my forearm. I probably won't be able to feel it anyway. I just hope I bleed."

Bob took a deep breath and held the scalpel to his arm. Jason nodded and Bob exhaled. Jason closed his eyes. Bob pierced the skin and slid it an about an inch down his arm, a nice clean cut.

"Do it already."

"I did. You didn't feel it?"

He opened his eyes.

"*No*. I can't feel anything."

Together they looked at the cut on Jason's arm as it slowly oozed one drop of thick black blood. The skin around the cut immediately bruised black and purple.

Bob started coughing and gagging. His fist covered his mouth as he continued to hack. Jason could see his eyes cloud over followed by a couple tears.

"It stinks," Bob choked. "Jesus, it stinks I'm going to…" he trailed off and didn't even make it out of the chair before he puked all over the floor.

Jason watched in horror as Bob wiped his mouth with the back of his hand and fished a surgical mask out of his bag. He tied it over his mouth and slowly regained his breath and composure.

"Your blood smells like a rotting dead body."

Jason flinched.

"Take it easy."

"Sorry Jason, but it smells awful."

"Why can't I smell it?"

"I don't know."

"What are we going to do?"

"You're going to clean up that puke and I'm going to step outside and call someone else for help. A specialist."

"A specialist? You mean people have seen this before?"

"I don't think anyone has ever seen this before, no. But, I guess he's as close to a specialist in this situation that I know of. Let me give him a call."

"Who is he?"

"His name is Willis," Bob said, walking out of the kitchen. "He's a mortician."

Jason shouted after him.

"Why do *I* have to clean up *your* puke?"

"Fascinating," Willis said. He was peeling back the skin on Jason's forearm with forceps, using his gloved fingers to test the tissue inside. Bob was several feet away, looking green.

"Give it to me straight, doc," Jason said smiling, "how bad is it?"

"Well," Willis said, looking up, "You've already passed beyond lividity and pallor mortis, and rigor mortis is setting in nicely. I expect we'll see discoloration, marbling, and bloat soon."

Jason looked at Bob, who shrugged with a look that said *not really my department.*

"Can I have that in English?"

"Certainly," Willis said. "You are decaying. Rotting. Yet, somehow you are talking to me. I find it … disconcerting."

"You and me both, pal. Well, what do we do about it?"

Willis just returned his look, saying nothing for several seconds.

"I'm not sure I understand," he said. "There's nothing we *can* do. You're dead, and your body is rotting. It's completely natural. Well, except for the moving around, talking thing. That's highly irregular."

"You can't help me?"

"I'm afraid not."

"Get out of my house," Jason said. Willis, with a nod to Bob, gathered his things and left without another word.

"Rigor mortis?" he shouted at Bob. "Fucking *bloat?"*

Bob shrugged. He looked contrite as hell. Jason wished Cal was still here and not at school. Hell, he even kind of wished Callie was here, too.

Bob stood up.

"Um. I'm gonna go. Okay?"

He had already put away his doctor gear. Jason's shoulders slumped.

"Yeah. Go ahead, man. I'm sorry I yelled at you, Bob. Been a rough day."

He smirked.

"No shit. For what it's worth, I'm sorry, too. I wish I could help you, but this is way out of my league. Maybe you should call a priest or something."

"I'm agnostic. I think. I'm not sure what to believe anymore."

Bob grinned and clapped him on the shoulder.

"If you're agnostic, you weren't sure what to believe in the first place."

Jason laughed.

"Get out of here, dick." he said. "Thanks for trying, man. Really."

Bob nodded and walked to the door. He paused, looked back at Jason one last time, nodded again and closed the door behind him.

Jason stood looking at the closed door for a long time. He had no idea what to do. He didn't want to be alone. He moved his stiff legs, heavy feet thump-thumping to the door. His clawed fingers fumbled at the doorknob and finally got it to turn. Jason yanked the door open and stepped outside. It was a crisp, sunny fall day. In the driveway, on top of his Fiat a shiny black crow stood. It cocked its head and shot him a look that seemed hungry. He stuck his tongue out at the bird.

"Fuck you."

He went back inside.

Four hours later, Cal walked in and threw his backpack down with a resounding thud.

"Dad?" he called without looking, "There are a bunch of birds outside. It's weird."

Cal turned and saw his father. The boy froze, mouth gaping. Jason's skin was a marbled yellow-orange; his abdomen was so distended he looked pregnant; he was grinning horribly without trying. Jason turned filmy eyes to his son. His voice, when he spoke was distorted by the rictus of his mouth.

"Hey, kiddo," he rasped. "How was school?" A loose tooth fell onto his dry tongue and he spat it onto the floor.

"Holy shit!" Cal said, turning green at the sight and the smell. Then he realized what he'd said to his father and his face tinged red. Jason thought his son looked like Christmas.

Cal started to apologize but Jason exploded with corpse gas from both ends of his body. Jason's bulging belly visibly shrank visibly .

Cal looked horrified but Jason just shrugged. He'd come to terms with his situation and after the day he'd had, a couple farts in unison were nothing.

"No sweat, son. I don't think bad language matters much anymore."

He rested his hands on his bloated stomach.

Cal gagged at the stench but quickly recovered.

"So what did Bob say?"

"What. Did. Bob. Say?" Jason sighed drawing the words out.

Cal just blinked at him.

"Well, Bob said that he thought I was dead. I didn't believe him so he called a mortician. That guy said I was dead too."

"Then how are you talking to me?"

"If I knew, kiddo, believe me, I'd tell you."

He looked down at his arms and saw that in addition to the cuts they had made on his forearms earlier, there were other wounds. Pieces of his skin were beginning to decay. He didn't know how he'd missed it until now, but a few maggots poked around from beneath the top layer of his epidermis and black flies buzzed and landed in little clouds around his exposed skin. *When did that happen?*

"So," Cal said, "do we need to call someone? Maybe Mom?"

"There's nothing anyone can do, especially not your mother. I'd hate to ruin her day with this kind of news. She was mad enough at me when she left this morning."

"Yeah but look at you."

"I know. And I don't want to hear another word about it," he said and immediately went into a nasty coughing fit. Teeth flew amidst pieces of something. Esophagus or trachea or some fucking thing. The teeth clicked and scattered, the tissue just kind of stuck in the spot it landed.

"Well, what do you want me to do?" Cal asked, unconsciously covering his mouth. "How can I help?"

"Honestly kiddo, I don't really know, but I'm sick of sitting in this chair and I can barely move. Can you give me a hand and get me to bed?"

Cal hesitated; he swallowed hard a few times.

"Uh, yeah. I mean, I guess so," he stuttered. "Just give me a second okay?"

"Sure," Jason said, and Cal left the room.

He came back a few minutes later and when Jason saw him, he couldn't help but laugh. He laughed so hard one of his eyes popped out and dangled down his cheek by the optic nerve. He tried to poke it back in, but it was too slippery, so he left it on his cheek.

Cal approached in a yellow rain slicker, yellow rubber gloves, puke-green wading boots, and a pair of swimming goggles. He had a bandana tied over his nose and mouth like a wild-west outlaw. His voice was muffled.

"Don't take it personally, Dad, but you're kind of gross."

After fighting off his raspy laughter, Jason realized his lips had split in the middle.

"No offense taken."

"Alright," Cal said. "Let's get you to bed."

With enormous effort, Jason extended his clawed hand. Cal grabbed it with one his rubber-gloved hands and pulled. Jason barely moved. With his stiff joints he was pretty much dead weight. He smiled at the thought, not that anyone would be able to tell past his rigor-rictus.

"Use both," he said.

Cal gripped Jason's hand with both of his and pulled with all his might.

With a sick rip, his arm came free at the socket in a burst of stench and maggots and stringy tissue but little blood. The sudden shift in weight knocked Cal backwards. He screamed as he fell on his ass. The arm flopped across his stomach and he panicked, tossing it to the floor.

"Looks like I gave *you* a hand instead," Jason said, hysterical, his hanging eye slapping against his cheek as he laughed.

Cal didn't laugh.

Cal was pissed.

"This isn't funny Dad. Jesus. Mom was right about you. You never take anything seriously. You're dead and I'm trying to help you and you're just laughing."

Jason coughed and laughed but couldn't form any words.

"Let's just try again."

Cal's serious tone stopped his laughter. He looked at his son and nodded.

"Sorry."

"Look, Dad. You're too heavy for me to lift. We'll have to make more than one trip."

"How?"

Cal put his foot on his father's ribs and took hold of the remaining arm.

"I'm sorry, Dad. I hope this doesn't hurt."

Jason shook his head. Nothing hurt anymore. Tears fell from Cal's eyes as he heaved. The arm came out of its socket with a slurping, tearing sound. Cal kept his feet this time; he set the arm by the other one. He was crying hard by the time he got his father's legs off.

He carried the limbs like cord-wood to his parents' bed and arranged them with room for the rest of the body, roughly where they would be if his father was still in one piece. He returned to the living room.

Jason was staring at the still open door.

"Cal, buddy," he said, "I might be in some trouble. I think now would be a really good time to tell you I love you."

"I love you, too, Dad."

He was about to say more when he heard the noise. From outside, it sounded like a thousand paper fans being shaken at once.

Crows, hundreds of them burst through the door. Most of them flew to Jason on the couch, covering him completely and pecking bits of him into their beaks. Fifty or so went back to the bedroom. The noise was incredible; the scene was surreal, insane. Cal covered his head, but the crows ignored him.

After a few minutes, the crows poured back outside all at once. Cal looked at the open door in disbelief for a few seconds.

He could see why they called it a *murder.*

He turned back to the couch. Nothing remained of his father but bones. The jaw opened once and closed again with a *clack.* He lifted the bones. Dad was a lot lighter now. He put the loose teeth in his pants pocket and brought his father's remains upstairs, laying them with the bones of his father's arms and legs that were also pecked clean.

"Mom's gonna see this and have a cow," he said. "If you're still aware somehow, you must be pretty pleased about that."

Cal looked at his father's bones on the bed. He was quiet for a long time.

"I gotta tell you, Dad, I hope this isn't hereditary."

Upping the Production Values

Martin French had loved horror movies since he was six. That year, his father took him see "The Creature from the Black Lagoon" in the theater; it had been his dad's favorite when he was a boy.

As soon as the creature hit the screen for the first time, he was hooked. He asked his dad to get him all the classics: Frankenstein, Dracula, The Wolfman, The Mummy. Martin's mother said he'd have nightmares, but he never did.

By the time he was fifteen, Martin was a horror movie expert. Plywood DVD shelves were bolted to the walls of his room, stocked with everything from "The Abominable Doctor Phibes" to "Zombieland."

When he was seventeen, Martin made a short horror film of his own: "Crushing Desire." It starred his friend Kelly, an eighteen year old senior and fellow horror fan.

The film opens with her wearing sweats and t-shirt. She is standing in a room that is empty except for a large box. She looks at the camera and smiles; she lets her sweatpants fall and puddle around her ankles. Kelly peels off her shirt; there's nothing under it. Looking into the camera again, she pulls down her underwear. She runs her hands down her naked sides and tosses her hair back.

She opens the lid to the box and climbs in. She somehow makes it seem sexual. She beckons to the camera which moves in on her. She closes the lid and squirms, touching herself all over.

She stops, eyes wide as the box jolts. Kelly starts to panic as the box gets smaller and smaller, beating against the sides with her fists until it slowly crushes her to death.

Martin built twenty eight identical and progressively smaller wooden boxes. She had squeezed into each until she could not fit in the last one.

The final shot was the outside of the smallest box; her voice-over screams faded to quiet as blood oozed out from the bottom of the box. Creepy music Martin had composed on the computer added disturbing ambience. He edited it to look as if the box was shrinking on camera.

He had entered "Crushing Desire" in a Detroit horror film festival. It won the audience choice award. His dad grinned and clapped him on the back; his mom left the theater after her son's film and wouldn't meet his eyes until the next day.

On his eighteenth birthday, Martin only got one present.

"Oh my *god.* A Hi-Def Camera. No. Way. You guys rock!" He hugged both his parents with the hand that wasn't holding the new camera.

Martin and Kelly were sitting in the Chicken Shack. He was drinking coffee; she had a chocolate shake that she was making last as long as possible.

"How would like to be in another film?"

"Martin, you have a real gift, you know that?"

"For what?"

"Well. Making movies for one thing," she said. "But, also you're kind of a born leader."

"I am?"

He didn't sound convinced.

"Last year, you convinced me to take my clothes off on camera," She tossed a mischievous grin at him. "I never thought I could do that, but you made it seem like nudity is the most natural thing in the world."

"That's because it is."

She shook her head, smiling.

"Well. Whatever this project is, you know I'm on board. I think you're brilliant, and I plan to ride your coattails to fame and fortune."

The waiter brought a thick, greasy cheeseburger, rare on a plate with waffle fries and a pickle. He set it in front of Kelly who thanked him.

"You eat that stuff?"

By way of answer, she hefted the burger and took a huge bite. Thin red juice dripped down her chin; she caught it with a napkin.

From his backpack, Martin pulled a sheaf of stapled pages.

"You wanna hear what it's about?"

She nodded.

"Mm-hm." Her cheeks bulged with food around her smile. He handed her the script and she read while she ate.

INT. *Dimly lit room, single chair in center, small window high on the cement wall. It is a basement, pipes running overhead. Water can be heard dripping slowly off-camera. MARILYN is in the chair, wearing a blue sundress. Her hands are tied behind her back, her feet bound to the chair legs; she is slumped over, unconscious. A* FIGURE *steps into frame wearing surgical scrubs. In the Figure's left hand is a straight razor, glinting in the meager light. Marilyn stirs, moans. The Figure shivers in anticipation.*

She swallowed hard and picked something out of her teeth. She didn't look up from the pages until she had read the whole thing.

"Oh yeah. I am so doing this."

Martin had written the part of Marilyn with Kelly in mind. A lot of directors use the same actors again and again. The male actor was new to them both; Martin knew him from film class, but hadn't worked with him before. He had written lines for the Figure, but James had a stutter; it was a bad one, and he couldn't do dialogue.

However, he looked great for the part; he was over six feet and broad-shouldered. He wasn't particularly muscular, but not fat either, just big. The lack of speaking lent the Figure an even more disturbing air; his stutter was a blessing in disguise.

It was just the three of them and Martin's new camera in the basement along with the tripod, lights, light stands, boom and microphone. He was running all the tech himself; he set everything up before the cast showed up.

He watched through the camera's small monitor as James lifted Kelly's head by the hair. The camera studied her face as the Figure did, and Martin thought she looked beautiful on screen, despite or maybe because of the bruise on her cheek and the burst capillaries in her eyes. Makeup and contacts, but it looked very real; *my makeup skills are improving*, he thought with no small amount of pride. He zoomed in as James leaned closer, his face almost touching hers. He inhaled deeply, smelling her skin. Tentatively, he stuck out his tongue and tasted her cheek. Her eyes widened and flicked in his direction.

"Please," she whispered. "Please. I'll do anything. Just don't hurt me."

He put his finger to his lips and shook his head. He pulled the neck of her dress away from her skin with his free hand and used the razor to cleanly cut it from her body. The blade was real; it belonged to Martin's dad. He had a prop razor that looked just like it on the table with the soda and snacks; later, they would use that for close ups of skin cutting, adding the blood in post-production. She held very still, watching the blade move inches from her skin. He sliced all the way down to the hem and through it; he peeled away the severed halves, exposing her bra and panties.

"Please," she said again. He ignored her this time and very carefully slid the blade under the bra at the join between the cups. The edge of the blade nicked her right breast, just a tiny bit, but it drew blood. He stopped; he, Kelly and Martin watched the trickle of blood as it ran down her ribs and abdomen.

That was not in the script. It was an accident, but it looked amazing on camera so they kept rolling. Everyone was still in character, maybe more so than ever. James carefully turned the razor blade so it was facing away from her and used it to slice the bra open. His free hand pulled away the separated cups, exposing her breasts. The blood was darkening the elastic on her panties, though it was slowing down and clotting already.

"I don't want to die," she said, choked with fear and desperation. "Please, I don't care what you do to me, but please let me live. Don't hurt me. I can please you, I know I can. I can be a good girl. You don't need the razor. I'll cooperate, I swear."

James hooked her panties with a finger, pulling them away from her hip. He used the blade to slice the fabric, then repeated the procedure on the other side. He went behind her, grabbed her underwear by the back and pulled them off, the camera catching the front of the panties disappearing between her legs. Naked, she began to cry. Martin tilted the camera up and zoomed in on her face; he even got an extreme close-up of one of her eyes as real tears fell. Beautiful.

"Cut," he said quietly, stopping the camera and immediately turning off the hot lights. "Wow." James sat down as Martin unlocked the cuffs and untied Kelly's ankles. She got up and reached for a robe, but Martin stopped her.

"You'll smear the blood," he said. "Sorry, but you need to stay naked. Are you cold? I can get the space heater."

"No. I'm okay. I wasn't thinking."

"K-K-Kelly," James said. "I'm s-sorry I c-c-c-cut you." He gestured vaguely at her chest.

She smiled at him.

"Don't sweat it, James. It hardly hurt at all and besides, it totally ups our production values."

"That's why I love this woman," Martin said. "She's a big-picture girl all the way. I need to do the second set-up; James, will you help me move these lights? They should be cool enough by now. Just don't touch the bulbs: you'll get burned and they might explode. Seriously. Also, they cost a fortune. Thanks. Right over there. Good."

It took about fifteen minutes to get everything the way he wanted it and the actors in place; that was the beauty of a script where everything happens in a single chair. He checked the battery life and how much memory he had left on the chip. He was good for at least another hour.

The new camera angle was low, pointing up; Kelly's left thigh was in the foreground, out of focus. Beyond it, her still-bloody breasts and face were visible. Martin had added more bruising on her arms and torso, mostly finger marks. He had also added several new cuts to her shoulders, abdomen and legs, though these were simulated with fake blood. She was once again bound to the chair. She and James were waiting; Martin just stared at them for several seconds, mind racing. He looked at his storyboards and them at the tableau in front of him.

"Ready?"

"I'm s-s-sorry, Martin," James said. "I s-suddenly have to p-p-p-pee."

"Shit. Go upstairs. Make it fast."

"No," Kelly said. "Don't, James. Stay here. Piss on me." Nobody moved or said a word for several seconds. James looked at Martin. He looked back at Kelly.

"W-What?"

"It fits the scene." Kelly's jaw was set.

"If you want Marilyn to be peed on, we can work that in, but I can fake it, Kelly," Martin said. "I think I have some Gatorade in the fridge upstairs."

"Just hit 'record', Martin," she said. "It will look better on camera if it's real. It's what the Figure would do, and you know it. James, you go ahead and do it. Martin and I want this film to be as good as it can be, don't we, Martin? Go ahead, James; I don't mind, really."

"This is fucked up, Kelly," Martin said.

"I'll d-d-do it. But you c-c-can't t-tell anyone."

Kelly smiled at him.

"It'll be our secret, James."

He looked down at himself. Martin hit *record.* James pulled down his fly and reached into his pants. Her eyes got wide as he pulled it out.

Martin watched in the monitor as James pissed on the girl tied to the chair. He started on her thighs, arcing up her belly and breasts then he pissed on her face. She whipped her head back and forth, trying to escape what was happening to her.

It was sick and fucked up and looked amazing on camera.

After, James went to the utility sink and washed his hands. Martin kept the camera on Kelly. Her head slumped. Urine dripped from her hair. The razor was on the chair next to her. The water was still running off camera.

She wriggled in the chair, pulling at the ropes holding her wrists. She got a hand free just as the water stopped. She snatched the razor and quickly put her hand behind her back.

James stepped into frame. Martin's heart was pounding behind the camera. He was still rolling. There 27 minutes left on the battery.

James, as the Figure, leaned over her. He flicked his tongue out like a snake.

Kelly's hand whipped forward. The open blade flew across his throat. Blood arced out and he jerked back.

He fell on his ass on the stone floor, holding his neck with both hands. His eyes were huge.

"K-K-K-K-"

His eyes glazed over. Blood soaked his shirt. She looked at the dripping razor in her hand and back to the big man on the floor.

Behind the camera, Martin swallowed hard. His throat was dry.

"Cut."

James fell back, limp. Kelly looked at Martin. Her eyes shone in the work lights.

"I already did."

"Jesus. What have we done?"

She untied herself from the chair. She set his father's straight razor on it and pushed her hair back. Stepping close to Martin, she smiled. He could smell copper and piss.

"We made a movie, babe. A real horror movie, just like you wanted. And you know what? I can't wait to do it again."

Martin turned off the camera and the hot lights. He stared at the body on the floor. The blood had stopped, but there was a lot of it. Kelly called his name from by the stairs.

"Can I use your shower? I'm a mess."

Impure Breed

Niles stood in the open back door of his house. He leaned against the frame and watched the alley. Clive had been gone for twenty minutes, which was ten minutes longer than usual. The dog's name was supposed to be a joke: Clive *Barker*. But, it turned about to be a girl dog, so people always asked why she had a boy's name. No one got the joke.

Putting his hands in his pockets and fiddling with the contents, he found a crumpled bill and pulled it out. George Washington looked at him sideways. The large *A* matched the smaller *A* at the beginning of the serial number. Niles had never noticed that before. Folding it in half, he slid it back into his pocket and looked again at the alley mouth. Clive was nowhere to be seen.

A scraping sound snapped Niles' head around. His dog limped toward home. He ran to her and felt all over, his panting matching hers as his fingers felt for wounds. He couldn't find any, but Clive smelled like rotten eggs and was favoring both her back legs. After a bath, she smelled like herself again but still seemed out of sorts.

The next day, his dog was still moving stiffly, so Niles called the vet. The woman on the phone said it didn't sound like an emergency, but that she'd be happy to look at Clive if he brought her in. The vet had an opening day after tomorrow. He had seen her at the office a few times; her name was Rebecca. Her long, burgundy-dyed hair framed high cheekbones and a slightly upturned nose; her eyes were the green of a tropical lagoon. For a doctor, she dressed casually, but well: designer jeans or pencil skirts and a button-down blouse. Every time he saw her he found himself smiling uncontrollably.

The examination room, a door away from the lobby, was decorated with animal cartoons and pictures of kittens and puppies. Clive lay on a small, high table in the center, listlessly wagging her tail. Rebecca talked to the dog while looking her over, explaining what she was doing in a calm, quiet voice. Niles found it comforting, too. After fifteen minutes or so, she scratched Clive behind the ears, gave Niles a smile that made his heartbeat stutter, and gave his dog a clean bill of health.

Within a week, the dog seemed back to her normal, healthy self. She lost the limp and was soon playing tug of war with the foot-long rope that was her favorite toy. She did seem to be eating a lot and putting on weight, but otherwise seemed fine. Until she started throwing up all over the house.

He brought her back to the vet. Signing in at the front desk, he joked that he wished he could buy health insurance for his dog. The young man with a lip ring gave him a tight smile and flat eyes.

"Very original, sir," he deadpanned. Niles frowned at him but kept his own mouth shut. In a lobby chair, stroking his dog's fur, he waited until the other guy wasn't looking and flipped him off.

The door opened to reveal the vet – skirt today – and he led Clive into the other room. Rebecca examined her for a long time, frowning and repeating the same steps over again before turning to him with eyebrows near her hairline.

"She's, um, pregnant."

Niles stared at the woman. Behind Rebecca's designer glasses she blinked those green eyes at him.

"She was spayed in this office," he said. "As far as I know, you were the one who did it."

"I was. And, I know. Technically, this isn't possible. A dog that has been spayed should never get pregnant. I've never seen or heard of it happening. This is basically a miracle."

He had no memory of the drive home from the vet's office. Going through the motions, he ushered Clive into the house and out the back door so she could relieve herself in the alley. The air was crisp and the wind carried hints of autumn through the leaves. Niles rubbed his upper arms with his hands and jumped a couple times. He let her in and closed the door.

"Have to turn on the heat, pretty soon, bub," he said. She wagged her tail. He fed his dog and thumped her ribs with his palm. Cracking open a beer, he slumped in his chair by the front window. Reaching for his book, a true crime novel he was struggling to finish, Niles glanced out the window; movement caught his eye, a dog-sized flash of pink in the fading light of dusk. He watched for a while, but saw nothing else.

The next month was uneventful. As the dog got heavier, she seemed to slow down. She spent most of her time lying near the heat vent, only moving to eat or go outside. In the alley, Clive would only walk six feet from the back door to relieve herself. Toward the end of October, Niles was helping his dog across the room; she was only four but moved like an eighteen-year-old dog.

On November first, as he was taking down Halloween decorations, Clive started whining loudly. He set down the cardboard skeleton and knelt next to his dog.

"What's going on, girl? Is it time? Are puppies coming?" He stroked her sides with one hand and scratched her ears with the other. She gave a yelp and jerked under his hands. Flatulence escaped her back end and Niles looked. Blood spattered the carpet behind her. He hugged his dog, stroking her fur and talking to her in a soothing voice. With another pained *yip,* she convulsed and gave birth.

He leaned over his dog to see the miracle puppies. There were three of them: tiny, fuzzy pink things. They looked like long, skinny Hostess Sno Balls with legs. Fuzzy, pink, stretched out tennis ball wiener dogs.

The creatures made tiny, pathetic mewling noises. He had never seen a dog give birth before, but even his amateur eye could tell these were not normal puppies.

Clive stretched her head around to look at them. Sniffing them, the dog sneezed. She shook it off, growled and grabbed one in her jaws. Whipping her head back and forth, she bit down hard and the tiny creature was in pieces.

"Clive, *no.*" He scooped up the two still-living animals and held them to his chest. She gave him a reproachful dog face and spat onto the floor the part of her offspring still in her mouth. She nudged it with her nose, but it was still.

Clive's chest hitched and she gagged. Her claws dug furrows in the hardwood. The dog coughed and sneezed several times, but seemed unable to draw a breath.

"Clive?" he asked, still holding the pink fuzzies to his chest. "You okay, bub?"

She was not okay. She convulsed again and blood flowed from below her tail. She wasn't getting any air.

She lunged forward, jaws snapping; it looked to Clive like his dog was trying to bite a lungful of air. She shook her head back and forth, chest heaving.

He set the babies down and held their mother. He cried as his dog struggled for air, but couldn't help her. In minutes she was dead.

Niles was on the floor, weeping softly into his dog's fur when he felt something. The little pink guys climbed onto his leg and nuzzled him. Holding the two helpless creatures to his stomach, he cried until he was empty.

Once, he could control himself again, he called the vet's office. After a moment, he got Rebecca on the phone. He told her what happened; he couldn't keep the tears out of his voice.

"Are the other puppies okay?" she asked.

"I'm not sure. I guess so, but I don't think they're normal."

"Niles, I'm about to go to lunch. Why don't I stop by to look at the litter? I can also pick up Clive and the other puppy for you so you don't have to - you know."

He thanked her and hung up. He put a throw pillow in a cardboard box and set the squirming pink furry animals on it. Without looking at his dead dog or the dead baby thing next to her, he picked up the clutter in the living room. There wasn't much; he lived alone and kept his place neat.

Twenty minutes later, Rebecca arrived with a dog carrier and a quart-sized Chinese food carton. She said hi, set down the food and with great care loaded

Clive and the dead pink newborn into the carrier. She closed it up and turned to him. He showed her the two living offspring.

"I don't think these are dogs," she said. "Whatever mated with Clive must have been really interesting."

She spent several minutes checking out the creatures and stood up, stretching her back. He surreptitiously watched her breasts push against her shirt pulling the fabric tight.

"What should I do?"

"Take care of them," she said. "Whatever else they might be, they're babies. Here. Call me if there's trouble." She handed him a business card from the office with a handwritten phone number on the back. "That's my cell."

She lifted the dog carrier; he held the door for her and watched her leave. She turned back once and he waved. She smiled at him and got in her car, sliding the carrier into the back seat.

When he was alone, he cleaned up Clive's blood. Then he tried to figure out what to feed his pink pets. They wouldn't drink milk or eat dog food; they didn't touch yogurt or raw hamburger. He noticed the carton on the table and opened it; inside was chicken fried rice. As the smell filled the room, the little pink guys mewled and swayed their heads toward him.

"You want this?" He squatted and held the food in front of them.

A slit appeared in the animals' tiny heads as they bent over the Chinese food. They slurped it up like fuzzy pink four-inch Dustbusters; there was about a pint in there and it was gone in about two minutes. They loved it. Niles grinned at them and made a sandwich for himself.

The animals grew fast. They were definitely not dogs, or at least not completely. Aside from the tiny mouth, they had no features on their heads. After two weeks, vestigial ear nubs popped out of the top of their heads. A week later, little bumps pushed through the space above the snouts; they might have been eyes. They craved a lot of contact with him and he often held them, humming lullabies.

Months went by. Niles spent a great deal of money on chicken fried rice. His pets always seemed to be hungry. He watched the fuzzy pink things get bigger and better defined week by week. They were larger than dachshunds after five weeks. At three months, the animals had grown to the size of pit bulls. Their eyes, which came in around that time were wide, shiny and dark brown. Their mouths filled with teeth, grinding molars in the back, needle-sharp canines up front. He got so many nips that he started to wish he owned stock in Band-Aid.

The animals' tails had grown, too: they were long sinuous things with a mind of their own, wrapping around table legs and making the animals stop short. The big pink quadrupeds were constantly having to untangle themselves.

One of those tails caught Niles around the ankle as he crossed the room holding a glass of water. A little sloshed out of his glass and fell on the one he called Sno. Part of the creature dissolved. There was a long pale scar where the pink fur was gone. The other animal, Pinky sniffed the scar, but Sno seemed okay. The scar never healed. Still, Niles was glad he hadn't brought them out in the rain.

"I haven't brought you out *at all*," he said aloud. The animals ate, but didn't create waste. "Maybe that's why you grow so fast." Sno unwrapped his tail from Niles' leg and made a *chuff* noise.

Most days, when he came home from work the big pink animals rubbed against him the moment he walked in. Since each of them out-massed him, this move pinned him to the wall. Their hot breath on his face smelled like soy sauce. It made his stomach rumble.

"Good news, boys," he said one day, grinning. He turned away from them to shake the rain off his umbrella. He called them boys, but there was no way to determine their gender. "I have a date. With Rebecca. *She* asked *me,* can you believe it?" Niles did a little victory dance around the apartment; the lion-sized creatures picked up on his excitement and dogged his heels.

He brought Rebecca home for the first time two weeks later. With her coat still hanging off her shoulders, she stopped and her jaw fell.

"They got *huge*." She finished taking off her jacket and handed it Niles. He accepted it with a gentleman's grace.

"This one is Sno," he told her. "And this is Pinky. You know? It just occurred to me: you and I are the only people who have ever seen them."

She put out her hands and let the animals sniff first. She tentatively touched one. Sno pushed against her hand and made a low rumbling noise deep inside. Pinky nudged her other hand, not wanting to be left out.

"They're so soft," she whispered, "Where'd you get their names?"

Niles shrugged. He smiled, a bit sheepish.

"Hostess Sno Balls. When they were born, that's what they looked like, remember? They're great, aren't they?"

"They're so cool," she said. She addressed the animals. "Yes, you are. You're the coolest." She petted one with each hand. "Hey, Niles, I'm starving. I haven't had anything since lunch. Can I raid your fridge?"

Niles nodded and pointed to the kitchen. He hung her jacket on the hook by the door. He idly scratched Sno and Pinky at the base of their heads, where they liked it.

"Oh, good. I love this stuff," came Rebecca's voice, muffled by the kitchen door. A chill crept up Niles' spine.

She returned carrying a cardboard takeout container and eating out of it with a fork. It was the fork with the bent tine that he never used because it always poked the roof of his mouth. The beasts went rigid under his hands. Rebecca's cheeks puffed out as she chewed.

"Oh no." His voice cracked. "Not that, please. That's not for you."

It was chicken fried rice. She lowered the container to her waist, one forkful still halfway to her mouth.

Niles gripped handfuls of fur in his fists. He shushed his pets. Watching the three of them, Rebecca slowly raised the fork.

"Don't," he pleaded with her. "Don't let them see you eat any."

Rebecca finished chewing and swallowed hard.

"What?" she asked. She raised her eyebrows, bemused and put the fork in her mouth.

He had no idea his creatures could move that fast. He was jerked off his feet and landed hard on his chin. In his hand, he held clumps of pink fur.

Niles looked on helplessly, his scraped chin burning as his animals pounced on his new girlfriend. Sno knocked her down and Pinky wrenched the carton from her hand. They both sucked up the food that fell out, leaving no trace of it. While they ate, each kept a paw on Rebecca; she couldn't move.

When the chicken fried rice was gone and the carton licked clean, both beasts turned their heads to Rebecca. The fork was still sticking out of her mouth. She turned her head to the right, keeping her eyes on the animals and let the fork clatter to the floor. Niles couldn't move; sweat trickled down his ribs.

"What's happening, Niles? What are they doing?" He shook his head.

Pinky lowered its muzzle and sniffed at her mouth. It looked at Sno, then sniffed its way down the woman's throat, her chest, her stomach.

Pinky made a *chuff* noise. Sno bared its mouthful of canine teeth in Rebecca's face and the crotch of her jeans went dark with urine.

"Oh god. Sorry. That's a fear reaction. How embarrassing."

Sno *chuffed* and both animals tore into Rebecca, using their needle teeth to rip her open. She screamed. Blood flew outward from their muzzles.

The beasts used their paws to pull apart Rebecca's flesh, to get to the chunks of rice, chicken, broccoli and watercress.

Niles stared, frozen; he was barely able to control his own fear reaction. It was a pink, fuzzy train wreck in his living room. The animals licked her clean, clearing away every trace of their favorite food.

When they finished, they turned their bloody muzzles to him. Their tails writhed, serpentine, behind them. There was no trace of the cute, fuzzy pink pets they had been moments before. They looked like Hell spawn.

He wiped his hands on his pants, took a deep breath and walked into the kitchen. He had to step over Rebecca's eviscerated corpse to get there. He tried not to get any blood on his shoes.

His pets followed him. They sat side-by-side on the tile floor, both heads cocked to the left. It would have been comical without Rebecca's blood on their faces.

Niles turned on both hot and cold taps full blast. He stood there watching the water for a moment. He cupped his hands in the water and splashed his face, once, twice. He yanked on the spray trigger and pulled its hose as far as it could go. He turned around, water dripping from his jaw to his shirt and he pointed the trigger at his pets.

Sno *chuffed.* Pinky *Chuffed.*

"I'm sorry guys." He squeezed the trigger and sprayed them both. They stood there and let him.

Pink, gooey sludge ran off the animals and into the floor drain. Both beasts whined in pain and confusion. They dwindled fast and in less than a minute, nothing was left except their eyes and teeth.

Niles scooped up the four brown eyes with a spatula and dumped them in the drain. He turned on the water again and ran the disposal; he listened to the wet grinding for a few seconds before turning both off. Silent tears fell over a clenched jaw as he worked.

He gathered up the teeth with his fingers, careful to hold the jaw by the back and not to touch the canines. He put them in the sink, too and washed his hands with dish soap.

He toweled dry and called the police.

"I've killed my girlfriend and would like to turn myself in," he said. He gave them his address and said he'd be home.

He returned to the living room and sat a few feet from Rebecca's body. He didn't look at the torn remains as he waited to be arrested. Tears flowed down his face.

When the cops knocked, he got up and let them in. When they saw the body, Officer James drew his pistol and pointed it at him. Officer Hardy put him in handcuffs. He didn't resist at all.

"I'm sorry," he said. "I didn't mean for that to happen. I really liked her." He didn't mention Sno and Pinky, his impossible pets.

Sitting in the back of the cruiser, he looked up at the dark thunderheads. He could feel the sudden pressure drop that preceded a storm.

Movement caught his eye from across the street. Something was crawling out from under Bill Madison's porch. As he watched, something large and pink slid out under the latticework, scraping its back and leaving a clump of fur behind. It was shaped like a dog, only bigger; its tail snaked out behind lashing whip-like. *He knows I killed his kids,* he thought.

The animal kept its gaze on Niles in the car, padding toward him on large, silent paws. He glanced toward his building. No sign of the cops. When he looked back, the animal was running. Above the car, lightning zigzagged across the clouds. The monster sped up.

"Shit!"

He slid across the seat to the driver's side and pounded on the bulletproof glass. The creature slammed into the cruiser; the door buckled inward but held. Its jaw slammed against the glass, yellow spit smeared by razor teeth, lips flattening out to show black gums.

His back against the door, Niles pedaled his feet on the seat, trying to get even further away. He heard muffled voices behind him and turned his head. The two cops were outside now, each staring at the pink monster and going for his sidearm.

The beast was clawing at the car now, leaving furrows in the steel. Niles could see the cops split up; Officer Hardy around the front of the cruiser, Officer James around back. They both shot the creature, but it didn't seem to care. It just kept trying to get to him. The passenger side of the car was caving in and the bulletproof glass was a wild network of cracks. The cops but a few more bullets in the pink monster. The roof of the cruiser began to give, the reinforced frame bending under the onslaught.

Thunder boomed, loud enough to shake the ground and everyone stopped. The cops, the monster and Niles all looked up. The rain poured from the sky like someone had upended a bucket. The cops were drenched in seconds and the pink creature bellowed and shrank. As it died, it still tried to get to him, digging its teeth into the door handle. In about twenty seconds, a pair of brown eyes fell to the asphalt. The razor-sharp canines dangled from the handle, attached to nothing.

The rain slowed to heavy and steady. Officer Hardy nudged the lone set of jaws with the end of his automatic. He looked in at Niles; a dark stain was spreading across the man's crotch, and shook his head.

"I hate this neighborhood."

What Little Boys are Made Of

Tina pushed down hard on the X-acto knife until it went through Martin's skin with a little pop. He whimpered through the balled-up sock, and tears fell from his eyes. With an exasperated sigh, Tina looked at her friend.

"You brought this on yourself, so you can just be quiet."

Leaning forward to add her weight to the blade, she dragged her hand down toward his belt, stopping at his bellybutton. Setting the bloodied knife aside, she pushed her fingers into the wound. Grabbing the edges and pulling them aside, she exposed Martin's innards.

Frowning, she poked around inside her friend's body cavity, pushing aside guts and organs. After a moment, she stopped and flicked the blood off her fingers.

Martin's eyes fluttered, fighting to stay open. They fixed on hers as she looked down at him.

"I don't see any 'snakes or snails or puppydog tails' at all," she said. "You are such a liar."

The Mummy's Curves

Except for that one thing, Dr. Wylie was a thorough, careful and competent archaeologist. Certainly, he had enjoyed a long and prestigious career in what was an often contentious field. That being said, the one thing was *significant.*

Once, Dr. Ernest Wylie's face had graced the cover of National Geographic. The morning his neighbor Carl walked across the lawn and handed him his advance copies remained one of the high points of his life. Despite the idiot mailman bringing them to the wrong house.

This bit of fame had come when he had unearthed a tiny stone dwelling in Sudan. It was in remarkable shape: complete with crockery, rudimentary flatware and a child's skeleton. The bones belonged to a boy who had lived almost seven thousand years ago. That discovery launched a three-month lecture tour, which paid well, but Dr. Wylie was glad to be done of it. He itched to be back in the field.

He had ancient artifacts to find, and he longed to mark his discoveries in his own special way. That aforementioned one thing.

The archeologist always insisted on being alone with his discoveries, immediately after they were fully revealed. He told his colleagues and students that he had to meditate on the profundity of the find and would tolerate no distractions. He knew they thought him eccentric, but he didn't mind. Far better they thought him odd than them knowing the truth.

Dr. Wylie, as soon as he was alone on a site, would take his penis out and rub it on, or if possible, stick it into the relic. This act got him harder than anything, including being with a woman. It was intensely erotic for him. He saw himself as *fucking* history.

After, he would entice to bed a star struck archaeology student, if he could find one; he would buy a whore if not. Sliding in and out of a woman, he imagined he could feel tiny particles of the relic creating electric friction. His orgasms were explosive.

He never lay with the same woman twice. He saw them as tainted.

Dr. Wylie and his team were on a dig in the southern suburbs of Amarna, not far from the house of the sculptor Thutmose, whose bust of Nefertiti is one of the great iconic images of Egyptian history.

Construction workers had been digging a basement for an office building when all work was called to a halt. The excavator had hit something made of hand-carved stone.

The machines were quickly removed and the builder was informed that this was now a historical site and construction was suspended indefinitely.

Dr. Wylie was there and setting up his gear within 24 hours. The first day, the temperature hovered around 100 Fahrenheit. Coolers full of ice and bottled water were placed everywhere in easy reach.

On the fourth day of the dig, they found a door. It took the better part of seven hours to remove enough dirt to see the whole thing. With great care, they opened it to reveal a tomb. It was tiny compared to most Egyptian burial structures: about the size a one-car garage. Inside, an intact mummy lay undisturbed among gold and jewels and artwork; Dr. Wylie recognized it as being from the reign of Akhenaten - father of the better-known King Tut.

Could this mummy be Akhenaten's lost bride, Nefertiti? The location certainly fit, as did the artifacts. If so, his immortality was assured. And, as a pleasant side-effect, he would likely be rich. Not that he wasn't comfortable now, but who wouldn't mind an extra couple hundred thousand to play with?

The fame and money were secondary, however. Dr. Wylie, PhD, renowned archaeologist couldn't wait to stick his dick in the mummy.

Most of the day was spent with the students cataloging the various treasures while he examined the mummy. He was almost certain it was female based on the morphology of the skull and pelvis. He put his hands in his pockets to hide his growing erection; when he could no longer wait, he ordered everyone out.

He gazed at the ancient, desiccated corpse lying on the massive stone slab. Gingerly, he turned the mummy over on her side. Throwing one knee on the slab, he pulled himself up. He yanked on the tab of his zipper, which got stuck halfway, infuriating him. Jerking it side to side, he blasted past the snag and pulled his thickening cock out of his pants.

Fully erect, he carefully pushed himself into the mummy's vagina, or the hole where it once was. It was dry and rough, like autumn leaves. This moment, this intimate contact with history was usually enough for him, and he'd withdraw, saving his ardor for the student or the whore. Not this time.

He felt something when he entered her. A barely detectable sensation of movement. If it had been a less sensitive part of his body, he would likely not have even noticed. It was almost as if she was responding, as if she were alive.

Slowly, he withdrew himself, but not all the way. When just the tip was still in the mummy, he slid back in all the way to the hilt. This time, he was sure. The mummy's dry vagina contracted to squeeze him.

He stopped moving. His scientific mind knew this was impossible. Yet, he *felt* it. He twitched the muscle that ran the length of his prick and waited. Pressure. *She's responding.*

He tried to look at the mummy's face, but he had turned her too far. Dr. Wylie leaned over to get a better angle, and felt resistance inside. Wetness, too, though from his own excitement or from hers he did not know.

She turned her head with a sound like crinkling paper. *She* was right. The woman's breasts were visibly filling out atop the ribs.

He stared at the mummy. Her face was still desiccated, but her eyes formed as he watched. Black as shadow, they looked back.

The woman's dry lips twitched at the corners. He couldn't move. He stayed in the same uncomfortable pose, leaning over her as her body slowly regained life.

Dr. Wylie never lost his erection; he stayed painfully hard inside her. Dried leaves yielded to mulch, then loam and finally warm, wet, velvet moss.

A leg that had moments ago felt like a stick slid, long, lean flesh across his chest and she lay beneath him, gazing up.

He held himself up off her and took her in with his eyes.

Deep brown skin; a rough black thatch of hair where his body met hers; that lovely little bump of a tummy; small but full breasts, the way he liked them; long, surprisingly muscular arms held now behind her head; face that was more beautiful than-

He gasped. He knew her.

"You're *Nefertiti,*" he said. "I've seen your bust." He blushed, looked down at her chest. "No. I mean. Um. You probably have no idea what I'm saying."

The woman didn't speak. She was fully fleshed out now. Her eyes brimmed with longing and her body moved.

He held his position, pushing gently against her and letting her have control. Her eyes never left his as she slid her pelvis up and down, riding him from below.

It felt great, but he was too aware of how bizarre this was. It made it hard to relax and enjoy. His professional mind also considered this a tragic loss: now he had no mummy.

She squeezed him inside her and brought his attention back where it belonged.

"I'm fucking Nefertiti," he mumbled. "I brought a mummy back from the dead with my cock." He shook his head, grinned like a kid and slid his knees to either side of her ass. This pushed him deep into her and she smiled like a cat.

He reached between her legs. He slid his thumb around his cock, dipping inside her to get it wet. He found her clitoris and drew slow circles on it as he brought himself in and out of her, matching the rhythm she had given him.

The Egyptian queen purred in her throat, her body writhing under his. Her hands came out from behind her head and she touched his cheek, his neck.

He rushed to take off his shirt so he could feel her hands on his skin. He lost three buttons in his haste.

Nefertiti caressed his chest and ribs. The man undid his belt and pushed his pants down, getting as naked as he could. He worked her clit with relentless gentle strokes. The queen cupped his ass with both hands and pulled him against her. She squeezed him inside her so hard it almost hurt.

"My God, woman!"

"Mmmm," she said. He needed no translation.

He lowered himself to kiss her. Her mouth tasted of cinnamon and allspice. Her tongue was lively against his. Her perfect breasts pressed against his naked chest. He pushed up again and watched himself slide in and out of her.

They locked eyes then and her mouth opened, breath coming in quick gasps. He felt her quiver around him. Wetness flowed over his balls. She slid a finger into his anus and he gasped in surprise and pleasure. No one had ever done that. Her finger moved a tiny bit deeper and he came.

It went on and on, pulsing out of him in waves of heaven. Nefertiti twitched her finger again and he pulsed into her once more, his whole body shuddering.

Dr. Wylie collapsed on the Egyptian queen. Their bodies were slippery with sweat and his heart was pounding. He tried to raise himself up to look at her, but she gripped his arm with her free hand. He could still feel her finger inside him, but now it felt awkward and uncomfortable.

"I need to get up, love," he told her. "We don't want to get caught like this, do we?" He smiled.

The woman spoke, but he didn't understand. He knew some Egyptian, but this was a dialect so old she might as well be speaking Cherokee. Her tone was clear though; it was haughty and venomous.

Suddenly, he flashed back to the old Hammer horror films where people who violated mummy's tombs met horrible ends. He hadn't believed in mummy curses since he was ten. Now, he wasn't so sure.

The woman licked his ear with a tongue that felt dry. He was still inside her, but flaccid now and his scrotum crawled with revulsion. The body beneath him became rough, but the arm holding him down was like a vise.

He could only see her shoulder, which was turning gray and desiccated before his eyes. He pushed against the slab with both hands, fighting her, but she held him tight.

The smell of chamomile and thyme filled his nose, too intense to be pleasant. He remembered that ancient Egyptians used them as herbs used to make mummies smell better. Mingled with the herbs was the smell of decay and dust. It made him sneeze, which made his sphincter contract around her now skeletal finger. He slid an inch out of her drying snatch.

His heart slammed against his ribs. He had to pull air into his lungs by force. His left arm went numb and he knew he was in trouble.

Still, the bitch held him down. He screamed in fury and terror as the woman he had been fucking rotted away with him still inside her. Inches from his face, Nefertiti clacked her teeth together once, loudly.

His's heart stopped. For a few seconds, his brain lived on. *This is going to look bad,* he thought. Then he died.

The Grunt

"You had sex with a *werewolf?*" Gina said. God, she was such a judgmental bitch. Why did I tell her?

"In *human* form," I said. "Besides, he was really very sweet. A total gentleman. And he was very attentive to my needs." My face grew hot.

"What if he had scratched you, for Christ's sake?"

That had worried me, too actually. But Gary didn't scratch me, or bite me. There was some licking, though. Rather a lot of licking. I could feel myself blushing again. *What? Am I fifteen?*

"I was perfectly safe, Gina. He didn't hurt me at all, and we used a condom." I left out the part where the damn thing ripped. We were so caught up in what we were doing that neither of us noticed until it was too late. But, I'm pretty sure you can't catch lycanthropy from semen. Gary freaked out way more than me about the rubber. I told him it was fine. Werewolves don't get diseases, so I wasn't worried about that. And, I was on the pill, so everything should have been totally cool.

Turns out, the pill failed. I was pregnant.

I tried to get a hold of Gary, but he had moved away. He'd said he didn't like to stay in one place too long. That he could control his Wolf, but someone always found out about it, and most people are touchy about werewolves. I didn't really care. I mean, if they're not trying to eat you — literally, I mean— what does it matter? I try to judge a person by how they act, and how they treat me. Gary was a great guy, and he never hunted humans; it was his rule. I felt awful that I couldn't reach him to let him know he's going to be a father.

Yeah, I was going through with it. I didn't really see myself as having any options. I mean, I've always supported a woman's right to choose, but there was no way *I* was going to have an abortion. I wondered if the baby would have Gary's eyes. I could remember them vividly, a blue so pale they were almost grey, tiny flecks of gold at the edges of the irises. I think, looking up into those eyes, I might have fallen a tiny bit in love.

The pregnancy was hard: fatigue; morning sickness; a constant ache in my lower back; swollen breasts that weighed twice what they used to. I was fat and ugly and gross, and I resented people who told me I looked beautiful or that I glowed. I'd smile and say "Thank you," but inside I was, like, *whatever.*

The first and second ultrasounds appeared normal. My obstetrician assured me everything was on track; my doula friend, who had nothing kind to say about doctors, told me I seemed just fine, too. But, in my seventh month, I started to worry.

My boy – he was unmistakably male in that second ultrasound - was pushing on my uterus hard. It hurt a little, and I was worried. I know werewolves are stronger than humans, by a lot and this little guy was half lycanthrope.

I asked both my experts about it, but neither had experience with a hybrid. The obstetrician advised me to let her know if I thought there was a chance of internal injury. She said that at this stage, premature birth was an option, and the baby would be small but viable. My doula, Hillary, said that boys especially liked to hit and kick, even before they were born. Hillary had a theory that it was evolutionary: boys were bred to be warriors or something. Seemed kind of sexist to me, not to mention far-fetched, but so did a lot of what she told me. Hillary was into astrology and numerology and some other -ologies, too, I was pretty sure.

The days grew shorter, and my temper paced them. Halloween was only weeks away. It was my favorite holiday, and I decorated for it every year. In a few years, I would be able to take my son trick-or-treating, but for now, I planned to dress as a pumpkin and hand out candy.

I had picked up three actual pumpkins, hoping to carve them over the weekend. I was on the screened-in front porch hanging the cardboard skeleton around eight. It was full dark already, but I could see the front yard by the streetlight. Three kids in their early teens (they call them "tweens" or something now) were whispering loudly and moving furtively from yard to yard. I saw one of them grab a pumpkin from next door, hoist it over his head and smash it in the street.

I put down the skeleton and hefted the shovel I still had out from when it was gardening season.

The kids snuck into my yard and I could hear their whispered excitement on finding one for each of them. I opened the screen door and stepped out, shovel held like a bat, ready to swing.

"You touch my pumpkins, and I'll smash your fucking heads."

The kids stood rooted to the spot for a moment, eyes wide in shock and fear. Grown-ups aren't supposed to behave this way, their faces said. Then, all at once they ran.

I lowered the shovel, nodding. That showed 'em.

It wasn't until much later that I realized how psychotic my behavior was. I sat, drinking tea before bed and wondered what was wrong with me.

At 35 weeks things got ugly. The Grunt - my nickname for the baby growing inside me: Gary's Runt: Grunt - was working me over pretty well. He hit me hard enough to bruise the surface skin, and it hurt like hell. I was worried I had internal bleeding or permanent tissue damage. I called Doctor Wells; she could get me in at three. I called Hillary; she said she'd be at my house in twenty minutes. Score one for the doula.

I lowered my bulk into a chair and worked my way through a ham and Swiss cheese sandwich. I never used to eat ham, but since I got knocked up, I couldn't get enough of it. Bacon, too. Really, any kind of pork product made me salivate. It was a good thing I lived in the city; if I were near a farm, I'd likely chase down and eat the pigs.

Halfway through the snack, ten minutes after I had called Hillary, the Grunt *changed.* I could feel happening it in my womb: limbs twisting, body shifting, face becoming a snout. I couldn't really *feel* those things, but that's what I pictured as the baby inside me became something else.

The previous pain had been a nice, deep-tissue massage compared to this.

The tiny wolf ripped me open from the inside. I fell off the chair screaming and smacked my head on the floor. Stars burst in my eyes and I was sure I'd pass out, but the pain brought me back.

My yellow maternity shirt was soaked with blood. The Grunt pushed his snout through my skin, stretching the shirt in the shape of a baby wolf's face. The

shirt gave, and his little head burst through the fabric.

My son forced himself the rest of the way out, wriggling to free his body of mine. I could feel his back feet pushing off my spine; the agony nearly made me black out again.

My blood spread out, soaking the carpet. *Damn it,* I thought. *That's never going to come out.*

The Grunt, fur matted with blood and vernix, clumsily crawled onto my chest.

The umbilical cord pulled taut against my ribs. He pushed his little Wolf face close to mine. His tiny tongue popped out and licked my chin. I tried to smile. Pretty sure I managed it. My son opened his eyes; they were a bright blue, not as pale as his father's, but lovely. They looked human, which was so strange in that tiny wolf face. They also looked sad, as if he understood what he had just done.

Hillary walked in the front door, which I'd left unlocked. Her scream was the second to last thing I ever heard. The Grunt's low hungry growl followed.

At least my baby would eat.

Danger's Balls

The amount of blood was surprising.

For a moment, no one moved or spoke.

"*Not the lens.*"

Gil Norman, Director of Photography on *Slow Bullet* would apologize for those words in both public and private dozens of times after. Defending the camera was always his first priority, but in retrospect, he admitted it was an insensitive thing to shout.

It took him hours of careful cleaning to remove the blood from the glass and surrounding mechanism. The lens was salvageable, though whenever he used it, Gil imagined he could still see a red tinge.

The accident was stupidly avoidable. Clay Danger (born Clayton Dupuis) did his own stunts - everyone knew that. It was a point of pride with him and the studio. It was one of the things that sold so many tickets.

Clay Danger was a living legend. From 18-22, he was on the front lines in the Marines, fighting for freedom in the desert. When he came home, he immersed himself in hand-to-hand combat. By the time he was 25, he was fighting full-contact, no-holds-barred pit fights for money. He won a lot. A talent scout searching for the next action star scooped up Clay Danger and threw him into a sci-fi thriller with aliens, guns, naked women, and more punches per minute than any film in history.

With his high cheekbones, square jaw and lethal combat skills, he rocketed to B-movie stardom. He took a page from Henry Rollins and kept his mind and body free of drugs and alcohol. He took two pages from Jackie Chan by doing his own stunts and bringing humor to his roles. Clay Danger was 34 years old and verging on making the A-list when he did his last stunt. His foot slipped on a tiny spot of engine oil and, instead of leaping over the whirling thresher blades as planned, he fell into them.

The tech guys shut down the blades in under two seconds and at first, from the side, it looked like he was unhurt. He lay on his back looking at the sky. He wore a mildly surprised expression, lips parted as if expecting a kiss.

Then, they saw the blood. The whole back half of Clay Danger was shredded to pulp. The chrome blades under him and for two feet to either side were stained bright red. Gil's camera lens had been shooting from a low angle and had caught the outer edge of the splash, prompting his infamous yell.

They rushed what was left of him to the closest hospital, though no one was holding their breath.

Benjamin Melkie sat on the edge of the bed. His spine was locked, a rigid line, and he kept his knees pressed together. The hotel room smelled like stale sweat and bleach. He kept his eyes glued to the picture on the wall. It was a flamingo standing on one leg in the water. Tall reeds made up the background. The glass before it was stained by the smoke of countless cigarettes.

The girl stepped in front of him, forcing him to look at her. Her skin was light brown, mottled in several places with paler, almost Caucasian tones. He knew there was a term for that skin condition, but it escaped him. That skin, so different from everyone else there, so different from anything in his experience, is what drew him to her in the first place. The bright yellow bra that pushed her small breasts together contrasted sharply with the brown and beige beneath it.

With effort, she peeled off her jeans to reveal a hairless slit. Above this, a pink Vagazzled unicorn pranced. It was missing an eye and most of its front legs, but it caught the light and sparkled. The pants were so tight the top button had left a circular indent in her skin. With a tentative fingertip, Benjamin felt the spot. He ran it back and forth twice, riding over the bumpy edges. His eyes were fixed on the unicorn and the smooth folds below it.

"I've never done this before," he said. Sweat dripped from his sideburns. His growing erection made him shift his legs, though he kept them together as best he could.

"I guess I'll have to walk you through it then."

Her speech was slurred, with drink or some other chemical. Turning red, he stammered his reply.

"That's not... I don't mean... I've done, you know, *this*, but, um, I'm married."

"Oh. That's okay. Lots of guys are married. I won't hold it against you."

The girl unhooked the clasp at the front of her bra and her breasts popped out. He looked at them, comparing them to Heather's breasts. The ones before him stood up well, he thought. When Benjamin had seen her in the bar, he had pictured her naked. The reality, while not the flawless image he had conjured, was still pretty great.

"Do you want to touch me?" the girl said. "Or, if you prefer, I can do all the work."

Gently, the girl pushed him back onto the bed. He lay there, staring at the ceiling. Superimposed on the white paint was an afterimage of a flamingo with pert breasts and a shaved unicorn snatch. Blinking it away, he laughed a little. The girl had his pants undone and was just reaching inside Benjamin's underwear.

"Something strike you as funny?" There was a hard edge to her voice, a dangerous edge. He felt his erection sag.

"No. Just, um, it's hard to explain." He tried to pull up his pants, but the girl's hand was in the way. She pushed his hands away and tugged on his prick harder than he liked.

"I'm sorry. This was a bad idea. I should go."

The girl shot him a smile. Her teeth were brilliant white; one of the top, front ones was slightly crooked. She shook her head no and dropped her mouth over him. His resolve faded as he stiffened against her clever tongue.

"Okay," he said. "I guess I'll stay for a bit."

The girl looked up at Benjamin and licked her lips. Pulling a condom from her purse, she slid it over him. Then, she slid herself over him, too. In under five minutes, he lost control and filled the rubber.

She gave him a grumpy look.

"I wasn't finished."

"Sorry," he said with a shrug. "Couldn't help it."

"How long before you get it up again?"

Laughing, he shook his head.

"I'm not in my twenties anymore. Sorry."

Wriggling off him, the girl scooting up his body until her glistening sex was poised above his face.

"Okay. Then you can go down on me. You need to make me cum. You owe me. Quid pro fucking quo."

She lowered herself toward him and he turned away.

"I don't, um, do that."

The look in the girl's eyes was flat and cold. It reminded Benjamin of the look he'd seen in the tiger's eyes at the zoo.

"You owe me, old man," she said. "You finish me off or I'll *take* payment."

He stared up at the girl, trying not to look at the two-toned cunt inches from his face.

"You're kind of scaring me."

"Good," she said. "You have no idea what you're missing, you know?"

Sliding a finger inside herself, she pulled it out and wiped it on Benjamin's upper lip. His nose filled with her scent and he jerked his head as far back as he could.

"You're crazy." In her eyes, Benjamin saw it was true.

"Don't you say that. Don't you *fucking* say that to me."

Pinning his shoulders down with her knees, the girl punched him in the face.

She hit like she did it a lot. He could taste blood in the back of his throat.

She hit him again, with the left this time. The blows kept coming and his eyes swelled shut around the vision of lovely, swaying breasts punctuated with painful jolts as her fists came down, one after another.

Benjamin thrashed under her, trying to buck her off, but he had no leverage. He blacked out.

He faded into consciousness. When his eyes slitted open for a second or two before he faded out again, he saw things.

The girl, still naked rooting frantically in her purse. The flamingo under its dirty glass. The glint of light off stainless steel.

She held his cock again, pulling and stroking. He had started to stiffen a bit when he felt cold metal on his scrotum.

White hot pain and a burst of warm wetness filled Benjamin's groin. His eyes opened as wide as they could and he pushed a strangled scream through broken teeth.

When Benjamin came out of anesthesia, he slugged the day nurse, knocking the man down and out.

"Vitiligo," he said. "That's what it's called."

The orderly who was changing the sheets in the next bed stared at him.

"Don't hit me, but what the hell is vitili-whatever?"

"I don't hit people."

"Okay."

He shook his head. His voice sounded wrong. He probed his teeth with his tongue. Five were missing or broken. He enunciated carefully.

"Vitiligo. It's a mottled skin condition, where a black person has white, well

Caucasian, patches. I couldn't think of it earlier. It was bothering me."

The orderly glanced at the unconscious nurse.

"Clearly."

Months later, after extensive dental work combined with an abundance of bedrest, he could again walk with hardly any pain.

With hardly a discernible limp, he stepped out onto the balcony of his apartment. Heather had thrown him out of the house, but he had seriously upgraded. He thought back to the last time he'd seen his ex-wife.

She had visited him at the hospital only once. She had sat with him for hours, reading a novel under the table lamp. She listened to the monitoring machines until he woke up.

When she saw his eyes open, she had closed the book.

"I want a divorce."

"Okay," he had said. It wasn't the resigned sigh she had been expecting, nor had he pleaded with her. This *okay* had been matter-of-fact.

"I don't even know who you are anymore," Heather had said. She left.

On the balcony now, looking out over the lights of LA, Benjamin sipped whisky, neat, and studied the swollen knuckles of his hands. He had never in his life gotten in a fight. Until a few weeks after the operation, that is. Tore out his stitches, but the other guy was worse of. Benjamin thought about the doctor's words when he went back in.

Clay Danger, he thought. *Clay Danger's balls.*

It was only six hours before Benjamin's catastrophic infidelity that Clay had fallen into the thresher. In that time, the unusual organ donation request was discovered in Clay's will. It was on video.

"When I die," Clay Danger had said, glaring at the camera, daring it to argue, "give my balls to a man who needs 'em. Don't fuck this up."

Veronica opened the sliding glass door and stepped out next to him. She wore a satin nightgown that the wind plastered to her skin, revealing the curves Benjamin admired so much.

"Hi, babe," he said. "Any word?"

She kissed his cheek.

"Vitiligo is not as rare as you might think," she said. "However, a search of dermatologists in town narrowed it down to nineteen cases, seven of whom were male. Only two of the females are in the right age range, so it has to be one of those. I printed the names and addresses and left them on the counter."

"Aren't doctor's records confidential?"

"I'm sorry. I thought you wanted results. Did you want to follow the law instead?"

He grinned and stroked her jaw with a finger. She visibly shuddered and a flush darkened her cheeks. He still marveled at his ability to make women go weak in the knees. *I shall only use my power for good,* he thought. *My good.*

"Thank you," he said, downing the scotch and handing her the empty glass.

At the first address, he was met at the door by a pre-school age child whose finger was industriously digging for treasure in one nostril. Benjamin grinned at the boy and asked if his mother was home. The boy shrugged and walked back into the house, continuing his uninterrupted booger mining operation.

"Who's at the door?" came a woman's voice from inside.

"Some white man," said the boy. Benjamin could see down the hall to what looked like a kitchen window. Pale yellow curtains hung limply over a sink full of dirty dishes. The mother poked her head around the doorframe. It wasn't her.

"What you want?" she asked without coming to the door.

"Excuse me," he said. "I used to know the family who lived here. They must have moved. Sorry to bother you."

"No family lived here but mine for a long time, mister."

"Oh? I must have the wrong house then. It's been a few years. I probably got confused. Have a nice day now."

Turning away before she could respond, he returned to his car and plugged the second address into his GPS. Twenty minutes later, he pulled up to an apartment building not far from the house he had shared with Heather.

Scanning the mailboxes, he found the one with her name. He waited. Twenty minutes later, a woman opened the door, a poodle straining against its leash.

"Let me get that for you," he said and held the door open as she led the dog out. He smiled at her and she returned it, holding his gaze for a long moment.

"Thanks. She's a handful."

"I can tell." Benjamin slipped into the building. He walked straight to the elevator as if he did this every day and pushed the call button.

On the fourth floor, he strolled down to apartment 418, home of one

Mandy Johnston, 23, college dropout, 'exotic dancer.' He knocked and stepped to one side so he wasn't visible through the peephole. After half a minute, the door opened a sliver. He shouldered it all the way open and pushed himself inside. He stood facing the woman who had cut off his balls. She wore a yellow sundress with white polkadots all over it. He flashed her his perfect, new smile.

"Mandy."

"Who the hell are you?"

"Now, that really hurts, being forgotten. Not as much as getting my balls cut off. No, sir. That hurt a lot more."

"You."

"Me."

"The fuck you want?

"You wanted me to 'finish you off', remember? 'Quid pro fucking quo' ring a bell? I'm here to do just that."

"What the fuck?" She took a step back, raising her fists defensively.

He closed the door with his foot.

"Oh no," he said. "This time, I'm going to do the hitting."

Benjamin Melkie hadn't been a fighter. The few times he'd been threatened, he'd either talked his way out of it or run away. Except that one time, some crazy, mottled bitch beat the shit out of him and mutilated him.

But, now he had Clay Danger's balls.

Mandy threw a fist first, a slow, powerful roundhouse with her weight behind it. He eased out of the way and clipped her face with an open palm. She looked stunned and just stared at him as a welt formed on her cheek.

She tried to hit him again, but he danced out of the way and broke her nose with an elbow.

She was no match for the new Benjamin. She could dish it out, but wasn't so good at taking it. Six good licks and she was unconscious on the floor.

He tied her wrists and ankles together with faux silk scarves and dragged her to the bathroom, tossing her into the white, claw foot tub. Moments later, he returned, carrying her purse, rooting through it as he walked.

"Ah. Here we go."

Extracting the straight razor, he sliced open Mandy's dress and peeled the halves aside. She wore white panties that were stained with old menstrual blood. He cut them off her. No unicorn this time. A triangle of brown hair instead.

"Now, I've studied some anatomy books, but to be honest, I'm not entirely sure I know what I'm doing here. But, I'll tell you what: I'll try to be careful."

Poking his fingers around her abdomen, he found a likely spot, shrugged and sliced deeply into her flesh. Her body jerked and she whimpered. Her eyes fluttered open and she looked terrified.

He backhanded her with his fist and she was out again.

"Lie down."

Making another cut on the opposite side of the first, he dug around inside her body until he found what he wanted. Pulling an ovary out of each hole he'd made, Benjamin severed them from the fallopian tubes and tossed them in the tub.

Standing, he washed the blood from the razor and his hands until there was no trace of it. Pulling a linen cloth from his pocket, he wiped his prints from the straight razor, the tub, the sink handles and the doorknob.

“There,” he said to the unconscious and bleeding woman. “You’re finished now.”

He retraced his steps through the apartment, wiping down anything he’d touched. Using the cloth, he lifted the house phone from its cradle and dialed 911, leaving it off the hook.

He pulled the door closed with the cloth, then pushed the elevator call button with it wiping his earlier print off in the process. When the doors opened, the woman with the poodle got out.

“We meet again,” Benjamin said. She grinned at him, blushing slightly. He felt her eyes on him as he walked away. He was two blocks away, whistling carelessly when he heard the sirens.

Starter Home

"Holy smokes," Leeza said. "We're getting *a house* for 26,000 dollars?"

"Twenty-six, five, but yeah." Ben grinned at his wife. He still wasn't used to *wife.* It had taken him a year to get used to saying *fiancée.* Sometimes, he tripped over introductions, mentally sifting through *girlfriend* and *fiancée* before finally arriving at *this is my wife.* Then, after the tiniest pause, *Leeza.*

Leeza, on the other hand, seemed to make these adjustments fluidly. He had never seen her hesitate or stumble. Over anything. It was one of the things he admired about her - one of many. Not the least of which was her inheritance which was going to pay for their house in full. There would even be about ten grand left over, which was good, because the foreclosure they were buying needed a lot of work. The previous owner had let a lot of stuff go for a long time.

In addition to the basement full of mold, the garage roof was caving in, the stairs were missing risers, there was no bathroom door and all of the appliances were missing.

Still, $26,500 was insanely cheap for a three bedroom downtown. Ben had a bit tucked away himself. Pretty much just enough for a fridge, a stove, and a washer and dryer. Between them, they should be able to make this their dream home.

After the four-day knuckle-biting, stress-factory ordeal of closing, the first thing they did was hire a locksmith to change all the locks. It was the realtor's idea. *You just never know*, she had said. Then, a company came in to remediate the mold;

a carpenter hung a new bathroom door and fixed the steps; Ben put a floor jack in the garage to hold up the roof until they could get a permanent fix. The heavy, telescoping steel rod was set just far back enough for them to park a car. They didn't though, just in case the jack didn't hold.

They spent almost a week, with Leeza's friends' help, deep cleaning the walls, stripping all the carpets (hardwood underneath - score!) and disinfecting every surface. The women came in each day and got right to work, buzzing around the inside of the house like insects devouring roadkill.

Finally, they started moving stuff in. Less than a month after closing, they spent their first full night in the house. The bed frame lay in pieces against the wall, and the curtain rod hung above the window like a skeletal limb. The master bedroom still smelled a little like bleach. They screwed like teenagers on the mattress and box spring on the floor.

After, they lay back and stared at the stucco patterns on the ceiling. From the corner of his eye, he could see her grinning.

"First nookie in the new house."

He laughed.

"Yeah. Good one, too."

She kissed him.

"They're almost all good ones."

"Almost?"

She laughed in her throat; it was a sexy sound.

"That's still a pretty good record, honey."

"All right. I'll take it. G'nite, babe."

"Night."

Ben decided he wanted to try to fix the garage himself, rather than pay a contractor. Their savings had taken a big hit already, and they needed to hold some back for emergencies. He checked out books from the local library, showing the clerk his Drivers' License with pride to get a library card.

"Just moved to town," he said. "Bought a house. It's a fixer-upper, but I kind of love it."

The young, male clerk favored him with a genuine smile.

"Cool. Welcome to the neighborhood."

They shook hands.

"Thanks."

Armed with his home improvement books, Ben stopped at the hardware store and bought a big box of drywall screws. Long ago, his father had told him, "Boy, you can fix damn near anything with drywall screws and a drill." He'd had a good cordless drill for years. It was currently charging on the kitchen counter.

Back at the house, he watched YouTube videos on how to fix garage roofs, so he could see it actually being done. Snatching his drill from the counter, he slapped the battery in place. With the box of screws in the other hand, he strode out to the garage.

He stood before it, arms akimbo, chin high. Cocking his head to the side, he raised an eyebrow and did his best tough guy voice.

"Let's do this."

Three hours later, he staggered into the sunlight. His hands and back were sore from drilling two-by-fours over his head. He blinked in the bright afternoon, pulled his T-shirt up and wiped sweat from his face.

When he opened his eyes, an old man was standing there. Ben jumped. The man held up his palms and smiled.

"Sorry, there. Didn't mean to startle you." He extended a hand, and Ben shook it. "Manny Jones."

"Ben Foster. Just moved in a couple weeks ago."

Manny nodded.

"Yup. Thought so. House has been empty for a while now. Good to see someone taking care of it again."

Ben looked up and down the short block.

"You live on this street, Manny?"

The old man shook his head.

"Used to. Lost my house. Foreclosed. Just visiting the old neighborhood. Reminiscing, you understand."

Ben was silent for a moment while he studied the other man. Manny met his gaze and held it. His eyes twinkled with what might have been amusement.

"Was *this* your house?"

"It was. Yes, sir. This was my house. Lived here for twenty two years. Came on some hard times and had to give it up. Sometimes, I miss the old girl."

"Listen, Manny, I'm sorry you lost your house, but I'm not sure I'm comfortable with you visiting. I mean, it doesn't really bother *me*, but I'm worried my wife might be a bit freaked out, you know?"

Manny smiled. His dentures gleamed whitely in the sun. He clasped Ben's shoulder with a surprising grip.

"No trouble at all, Ben. I won't come around anymore. Just, like I said, reminiscing today. You won't see me again. No sir."

He turned without another word and ambled down the driveway, turning the corner without looking back. Ben stood in front of the garage for a full minute, staring at the space where he had last seen the other man. He shook his head.

"Okay. That was ... different."

When Leeza got home, he was showered and slathering peanut butter on toast. She kissed his cheek as she slid by.

"Mmm. Smells good. Did you fix the garage?"

He replied around a mouthful.

"Partly. I'll do more tomorrow. How's your mom?"

"Better. Still on pain meds, which make her pretty loopy. I'm tellin' ya, you haven't lived until you see your own mom stoned out of her mind. Hilarious."

He chuckled.

"I bet. I had a weird thing happen today."

"Yeah?"

"Yeah. The previous owner stopped by. Said he was in the neighborhood. Seemed harmless enough, I guess. Old guy. Still, it was, I don't know, uncomfortable, I guess."

She leaned on the doorway to the dining room.

"I bet it was awkward. Why do you think he would come back?"

"I don't know, honey. He said he lived here for over twenty years. I guess he's having trouble letting go."

"I guess he should have kept up with his payments then, huh?"

"Whoa. Harsh."

"Hey man. My mom nearly died. I'm allowed to be snarky. Also, this is *our* house now. I'm not sharing with anyone but you."

"And maybe, someday, a kid or two."

She smacked his ass.

"Maybe. Still on the fence about that. I'm okay with practicing, though."

"Right now?"

"You have other plans?"

"No, ma'am."

Putting the plate in the sink, Ben whipped his shirt off and reached for his belt. Leeza laughed.

"We can go upstairs first, big guy."

He kept undoing his belt, and let his pants fall to the floor. Her eyebrows shot up.

"Or," he said, already hard, "we could do it right here."

"On the table?" He nodded. "Scandalous."

Reaching under her sundress, she wriggled out of her underwear. She slid her butt on the dining room table and spread her legs. He positioned himself, but she wasn't ready. He groaned. Gently, she pushed him back.

"Hang on, big guy. There's some coconut oil in the pantry."

She grabbed the jar, opened it, and ran some oil over his prick. Then, she rubbed it on herself and got back on the table. He slid inside her effortlessly.

"Whoa. That stuff is amazing."

She squeezed him with those magical muscles and grinned.

"You're amazing," she said.

"No. You are."

"Mm-hm. Less talk. More movement."

He obliged her. After a while, the movement got so intense, the whole table inched across the floor. By the time it hit the wall, their breath was coming in gasps. He was palms down on the table top, driving into her. Her nails dug furrows into his back.

He threw back his head and exploded inside her. She came too, gripping him around the waist with her legs. When she had caught her breath, she nibbled his earlobe and whispered.

"We should do it on the table more often."

"Mmmm."

Ben leaned away a bit and brushed a lock of hair behind her ear. Movement at the window caught his eye.

Standing outside, watching them, was Manny Jones.

"*What the-*" Ben scrambled for his clothes, pulling on his pants as fast as he could.

Leeza looked outside and quickly slid off the table, holding down her dress. Her voice bordered on hysteria.

"Call the police, Ben."

Manny stepped back from the window and out of sight.

By the time the cops came, the old man was long gone. Ben told them who it was, that he had introduced himself in the driveway.

The officer did a quick search on his dashboard computer and came back to the couple.

"Sir, I'm sorry to tell you, but we can find no record of a 'Manny Jones' or 'Manuel' or 'Manfred' or any other derivations of the name in our database. It says here the previous owner of your house was one 'Beverly Chow,' now a resident of Fairbanks, Alaska."

"Then who was the old guy peeping Tom?" Leeza asked.

The cop shrugged. He handed Ben a card.

"If you see him around again, please give us a call."

They got in the car, turned off the lazy blue flashers and drove away. Ben stared at Leeza. He could still smell her on himself and wondered briefly if the cops had, too.

"If he's not the previous owner, who the heck is he?"

She shook her head.

"I don't know. What have we gotten ourselves into here?"

Ben forgot about the garage roof. Instead, he spent his free time on the laptop, searching for the house's history. Before Beverly Chow, the owner was someone named Stuart Wallace. Stuart apparently moved to Cleveland fourteen years ago.

There were twenty-seven Beverly Chows on Facebook, none of whom lived in Alaska. There were a ton of Stuart Wallaces, but most of them lived in the UK. One lived in Cleveland. Ben shot him a message: *This is a little weird, but I think I bought your old house in Michigan. Do you know a guy named Manny Jones? He'd be in his 60s, maybe early 70s. Thanks.*

He left the computer open and hit the kitchen to start water for Ramen noodles. He tore open the package and removed the spice packet. While the water heated to a boil, Ben sliced a hot dog into bite-sized chunks. Once the noodles were done, he mixed in the flavor dust and the dog. Then, he drained most of the water and ate it with chopsticks. He only ate this when Leeza wasn't around. The one time she'd seen it, she'd threatened to puke. But, he had started this in college and it was his favorite snack, his comfort food.

His computer pinged. He had a message window open on Facebook. From Stuart Wallace.

Hi. Thanks for asking, but I'm Stuart Jr. We did used to live in Michigan, but I don't know anyone by that name. Also, my dad's been missing and presumed dead for the last fourteen years. Not telling you this to freak you out. We've pretty much come to terms with it. But, I thought I'd save you the trouble of trying to track him down. Wish I could be more help. Good luck!

"Fourteen years." He took a bite. "Mm. That's when Stuart Senior lived here."

He did a quick internet search for Beverly Chow and Fairbanks, Alaska. The one relevant hit was an article in the local paper, which had since gone out of business like so many of them. It talked about how Beverly, a well-known advocate for the homeless families in the area, had suddenly up and left for Alaska. The director of one the charities with whom she worked was quoted as "...quite shocked, really. She was so involved, so passionate about helping people." Apparently, Beverly had asked the man who had bought her house to leave word that she had a sick sister in Fairbanks and was going to stay with her "indefinitely."

The man's name was listed as Manny Jones.

"Son of a gun."

When Leeza got home, he showed her what he'd found, along with the house's owner *before* Stuart, one Winston Garrett. She said he sounded like a cowboy. He agreed. No one had seen or heard from Mr. Garrett since he allegedly left Michigan nineteen years ago.

"So, let me get this straight: the last three people who owned this house, at least, have disappeared under seemingly mysterious circumstances?"

"That's what it looks like, yeah."

"You think Manny Jones did something to them, don't you?" He nodded. "You think he killed them?"

"Yeah. I do."

"What are we gonna do?"

"I'm gonna call my cousin Greg."

She gave him a blank look.

"Not really following you there."

"You haven't met him yet. He lives in Detroit. Does construction, mostly demo, smaller jobs. He owns a Bobcat."

"Ah. Right. Sure. Nope. Still have no idea what you're talking about."

He laughed.

"Baby, how would you like an in-ground pool?"

"Um, I guess. I mean, it would be great for the four months out the year we could actually *use* it. How does this relate to the whole 'disappearing persons' thing?"

"I bet he buried them in the backyard."

She glanced in that direction.

"I was going to start a garden back there."

"I'm not really suggesting we build a pool. Just that we pretend to be, so we can justify the digging. Then, if we find human remains, which I bet we will, we call the cops again, they catch this psychopath and we live our lives in our dream home."

"Only mildly haunted by the ghosts of the quite possibly murdered previous owners."

"Yeah. Potential drawback, I admit. But, hey. If it's haunted, we could charge admission and be famous."

"I think I'd rather have a pool."

"Yeah. I'll call Greg. See if he can come out. Okay?"

She nodded. They were quiet for a moment.

"Ben?"

"Yeah?"

"This is pretty messed up."

He pulled her close and stroked her hair.

"I know."

Gregg texted him back. He would be free this Sunday afternoon. Ben thanked him and set out for the garage, drill in one hand and a box of screws in the other.

He leaned over on the six-foot stepladder, trying to reach as far as he could before getting down to move the whole operation. He passed the tipping point by only an inch, but the ladder started to go. He wind milled his arms, trying to correct, but kept going. Gravity was going to win.

Suddenly, he stopped falling. He was upright. Manny Jones held the ladder, smiling up at him.

"Careful there, young man. You almost went over. Good thing I happened by when I did."

Ben swallowed. Several accusatory things to say to the old man crossed his mind, and he discarded all of them. The guy's hands were still on the ladder. Ben nodded.

"Guess it is. Thanks."

Not taking his eyes off Manny, he climbed to the garage floor. The drill, pointing down, felt like a pistol in his hand. His left hand clutched several loose screws. The ridges dug into his palm. It hurt, but he didn't let it show on his face. Instead, he smiled, super-friendly neighbor guy.

"You're back to visit again. I thought you said you wouldn't come around."

Manny shrugged.

"I was just passing through, running some errands. Thought I'd say 'hi'. I wasn't going to. But, hey. Glad I did. Hate to see you get hurt."

"Appreciate that."

The drill buzzed to life as Ben inadvertently squeezed the trigger. Both men looked at it. They laughed.

"Guess I forgot I was holding it."

"Guess so."

For a moment, no one spoke. A woodpecker beat the hell out of a tree in a nearby yard, its strong beak machine-gunning holes in the wood, looking for bugs to eat. Manny's eyes danced with what looked like mischief.

"That's a Pileated Woodpecker. Stake my life on it. Big sons-of-bitches. Native to here. One of 'em pretty much destroyed my cherry deck when this was my house."

Ben glanced at the back of the house, where the lawn met a line of gravel under the eaves.

"I don't see a deck."

"You see?" Manny was almost shouting. He flashed his too-white dentures. "Fucker destroyed it."

"I'm not really comfortable with that kind of language, Mr. Jones. I think maybe you should go."

The laughter in Manny's face was gone, like someone had flipped a switch. He stepped in close.

"You're not comfortable ... I thought you were a *man*, Ben. What you got in your pants there, a hole? A pussy?"

Manny's big-knuckled hand was suddenly between his legs. He grabbed Ben's balls, squeezing just a little.

He didn't think. By reflex, he swung the drill, hitting Manny in the side of the head. The old man took it. His head rocked a little from the impact. A small trickle of blood ran down his cheek. He squeezed Ben's nuts a little harder, though still just shy of pain.

"That'll cost you, Benny, my boy. And yet, I am glad to see that you have some balls after all. Good. You're going to be needing them. Be seeing you. Pretty soon, I think."

He let go and backed out of the garage. Halfway down the drive, Manny turned around and walked away, a man without a care in the world.

Ben waited a long time for his breathing to normalize. Manny was long gone by the time it did. He eyed the drill in his hand, half-expecting to see blood on it. There wasn't any.

"Damn."

He laughed at his own profanity.

"Oh wow. That's not like me. Not like me at all."

When Leeza got home, he told her about the garage incident. She didn't take it too well.

"He *touched* you? There? And, you hit him in the head with a drill? Oh my gosh, Ben. This has gotten out of control."

"The part that worries me is that he said it would cost me. I think he's going to come back again, for some sort of revenge."

"We'll call the police."

He shook his head.

"They can't watch the house all the time. They have better things to do, I'm sure. No. We'll just be careful. Greg is coming in two days. We'll wait and see what he finds before we involve the police."

"I guess. I don't much like it though."

He put his arms around her. She rested her cheek on his shoulder.

"I don't like it either, baby. But, I'm not gonna let this old man intimidate me. How scary can he be? He's like, seventy."

She laughed, but it was forced.

"Just be careful. It's not a good idea to underestimate people. He seems like he might be a little crazy."

"More than a little. You haven't met him."

She shuddered against him.

"I don't want to."

"He gets under my skin, Leeza. In the garage, I *cursed*."

Her eyes popped.

"We agreed not to do that."

"I know. It won't happen again. I'm sorry. I know how much you hate it."

She stared at him like he was something smelly stuck to her shoe. Finally, she nodded and no more was said about it.

Saturday morning started with thunder, followed by torrents of rain that lasted most of the day.

Ben hung brackets on the wall in the room that was going to the study. The wire shelving was propped against the desk. After an hour's work, he had the shelves attached. He stretched his spine, glanced at the boxes of books waiting to be unpacked, and stuck his tongue out at them.

"Later. Maybe. Hungry now."

The books had nothing to say to this, so he went downstairs to see what Leeza was up to and to grab some lunch. She was nowhere to be found on the first floor. She hadn't come upstairs while he was up there, so he glanced out back. He could barely make out the fence bordering the neighbors', but no wife back there either. She wasn't out front. He opened the basement door and poked his head around the corner.

"Honey? You down there?"

No response. He turned toward the kitchen and stopped.

Manny Jones stood, not three feet away, dripping rain water on the hardwood floor. He held Ben's cordless drill in his right hand and a vicious smirk on his face.

"Hi, Benny. She's down there all right."

Ben opened his mouth to tell him to get out, but Manny hit it with the drill, knocking out two teeth. Pain shot through his head. His hands flew to his mouth, fingers exploring the damage.

Manny hit him again, in the temple this time. And a third time. He crumpled to the floor, unconscious.

When he came to, his shoulders ached. He couldn't feel his feet or hands. Lifting his head, he banged it against something hard. His chin dropped again, and he lifted it more carefully.

He was in a strange room. The ceiling was low, six-and-a-half feet at most. The walls were dirt or clay. Basement or root cellar, maybe. The space high on the wall where the small rectangular window should be, was covered in a row of foam shaped like the inside of an egg carton. The whole space, roughly fifteen feet square, was lit by a single, compact florescent bulb hanging from a short cord.

Leeza lay on a workbench, hands tied together above her head, feet at each corner, ankles tied to the steel legs supporting the bench. She was wearing only her bra and underwear. Glancing down, Ben saw that he, too, had been stripped to his drawers.

Behind him, a door opened, letting in more light. It made a sucking noise, like someone breaking a Tupperware seal. He heard it shut firmly behind him. He felt the air pressure equalize again.

Manny, still holding the drill, held up his left hand, showing Ben a small pile of drywall screws.

"Had a headache for a while after you thumped me. That's what decided me, you know? I have to admit, I was on the fence for a while. You seem like nice people, and I really am getting kind of old for this sort of thing."

"Why are you doing this?"

Manny gestured vaguely with the drill. He pursed his lips, shrugged.

"This is my house, Ben. It was mine first. I had it built back in the day, when I was flush with cash. But, I did some bad things, and I got caught, pretty much due to my own stupidity. Live and learn, I guess. Went off to prison for a time. Lost my house. Some woman bought it. She was a, what's the word? Horticulturist. Plants. Turned my whole damn yard into a garden with flowers and all kinds of things."

Manny paused, held up a screw, turning it this way and that, and looked Ben in the eye. He put the tip of the screw in the center of Ben's palm on his left hand. Looking that way, Ben was unsurprised to see that he was tied to the support beam by his wrists.

Manny set the Phillips drill bit carefully on the flat part of the screw, lining up the "X". He pulled the trigger and leaned into it, driving it through the hand and into the wood.

Ben howled in agony. Leeza woke up, saw what was happening, and she screamed, too.

Setting a second screw in Ben's right palm, Manny repeated the process. More screaming from man and wife.

Setting down the drill and the remaining screws, Manny clapped his hands loudly. Once, twice, three times.

"Yeah. That's right. The show has begun. Thank you. Thank you very much, ladies and gentlemen."

Ben and Leeza went quiet. They looked at him, at each other. This guy was nuts. Tears fell from Ben's eyes. His hand throbbed hotly.

"Go ... away."

"Oh, for fuck's sake, Benjamin," Manny said. "Is that the best you can do? I just put drywall screws through your hands. Where's your fire, boy? Rage against me. Cuss at me at least, son."

He looked at the floor.

"I can't. I promised."

Manny shrugged.

"I do love a challenge."

Saliva hung in a strand from Ben's lip. Snot bubbled in one nostril. He glared at Manny.

"I hate you."

"I know. But, you're gonna hate me a lot more pretty soon." From a pants pocket, Manny extracted a box cutter. Ben's eyes went wide. "Oh, don't worry. This isn't for you. Although…"

Manny cut the cords binding his hands. His weight fell, only supported by the drywall screws. His face contorted in renewed anguish.

Manny turned away from him and slid the blade under Leeza's bra, in the middle, careful not to nick her skin. He sliced it upward and the cups fell away.

"Oh, hello. Now, these are some of the nicest titties I've seen in a long time."

He leaned over and flicked a nipple with his tongue, back and forth, until it was hard. Then, he took it in his mouth and gave it long suck. Moving back, he released it with a "pop".

"Yum. Let's see what we've got downtown, shall we?"

The box cutter slid under the cotton of her panties, stretching it tight before it severed the threads. He repeated this on the other side, then peeled back the remaining fabric flap to reveal her crotch.

"Now, this is what I like to see: a well-groomed pussy. Not a whole bunch of hair all over the place, but not shaved either. I do not understand this trend these days. Makes a woman look like she's only nine years old. I'm sure it appeals to pedophiles, but I like a woman with some *fur* down *thur*, if you know what I'm sayin'. Seriously, the bald thing, it's repulsive."

Ben sobbed, one huge, gasping wounded animal cry.

"Please, I'm begging you, don't hurt her."

"I'm not gonna hurt her, Bennie. I'm gonna be nice and gentle and I'm gonna lube it up first so it goes in smooth. She's gonna like it, you'll see."

Leeza squeezed her eyes shut.

"Fine. If you're going to rape me, just get it over with. I'll do it however you want, if you'll just let us go after."

Ben gasped.

"Leeza, please-"

Manny opened a drawer under the workbench. From it, he pulled a can of WD-40. He spent some time spraying the business end of the drill, covering it thoroughly. They both watched him. He turned the nozzle around, pointing it between her legs. He shot a jet of engine lubricant all over her labia. It glistened in her pubic hair.

"You didn't think I was gonna fuck you with my own dick, did you? Shit. That horse has long since banged its last filly. Nope. Nowadays, I have to use power tools to satisfy my lovers."

She squirmed, trying to avoid the drill as it loomed toward her, but the clothesline holding her down had precious little give.

She gasped when the cold steel of the Phillips bit touched her clitoris. With utmost care, he gently squeezed the trigger, just enough to rotate the bit slowly around. He kept it barely touching her, spinning lazily. The small engine's vibrations hummed through the steel bit, providing intense pleasure despite her terror.

He kept it up, flicking his gaze from between her legs to her face, occasionally glancing at Ben, who looked horrified. Yet, he watched. He was getting hard despite himself. After a few minutes, she came. It looked to Ben like a small orgasm, nothing earth-shattering. Part of him hated her for it just the same. While she was winding down, catching her breath, Manny undid the drill bit with a quick twist. He pushed the bit-less drill inside her, stretching her vagina.

"Ow."

"Sh. I know."

He worked it in an out, not using the trigger, until she opened up, taking it in. Her hips raised an inch; it was all they could. She bit her bottom lip and moaned. He pushed a bit further. The whole end was now inside her. Manny leaned over so he could see her face. It was rapt.

He pulled the trigger. Inside her vagina, the drill spun at high speed. The outer ring, rough so one could grip it to change bits, whipped its jagged edges across the soft inner tissue.

Her jaw dropped. Her eyes bulged. She shrieked and thrashed against her bonds. Her cries echoed off the walls, reverberating in Ben's ears. Finally, her voice gave out, though her mouth still stretched wide, screaming silently.

Manny nodded. He leaned back and pulled the drill out, still running at top speed. Blood spattered him, her, the walls and ceiling. A large drop hit the light bulb, casting part of one wall in a pinkish tinge.

She jerked as the tool withdrew, then she went limp.

"You killed her, you, you, *freakish psycho*."

Wiping blood from his chin, Manny faced him. He inserted the Phillips end into the bloody drill and tightened it. Picking a drywall screw up off the floor, he hunkered down in front of him With a gnarled finger, he flicked Ben's prick through his tighty-whiteys.

"She's alive. Still hard, huh? Seems you like the sick stuff, buddy. Wouldn't have guessed it of you." He torqued the bit, and wiped the blood on his pants. "Learn something new every day."

Ben blushed from his forehead to his collarbones.

"I-I can't help this. It's biological."

Manny nodded. He positioned the screw at the top of Ben's left foot. With his knees, he positioned Ben's right foot behind the left. Putting his shoulder into hit, he drilled the screw through both feet and into the base of the support beam.

Ben gave one short screech, followed by sobs. Slowly, and with much noisy popping of joints, Manny got to his feet.

"Let me tell you a story, Ben, my boy. Back in the day, before I got in trouble, I was a cool customer indeed. I was a sound engineer. You know what that is? I did the sound for bands. Rock bands, mostly. I even worked on the crews that recorded Iggy Pop and MC5. Got the meet the guys for a minute on a cigarette break.

"Yes, sir. I was super-cool back then. Also, I learned how to soundproof the absolute shit out of a room. That's why you and the missus here screaming doesn't bother me a bit. This part of the basement, originally intended to be a wine cellar if you can believe it, doesn't exist on the floor plans you saw when you were house-hunting. No one has ever seen it except for me and the seven other previous 'owners'. And they only saw it for a couple hours each." He chuckled. "And not one of them is talking much these days."

Ben snuffled snot up into his nose. He *horked* it up and spat, nailing Manny's shirt.

"What do you want? Why do this?"

Manny picked up a rag from another workbench drawer and calmly wiped off the mucus.

"I wasn't done with my story yet, Benny.

"So, here I was, super-cool sound guy, hanging out with rock stars, dating a beautiful chick – the one who wanted a wine cellar in her basement, don't you know – and generally living large.

"And, then one day, I come home, right upstairs, in the exact spot where you put your own king-sized bed, and see my fine chick with another man's dick in her mouth. She's buck naked, ass in the air, going to town on this guy's cock. Wet, slurping thumps hit her throat as she took him all the way in. I could hear it from the doorway.

"Well, sir. I guess I kind of lost it. I used to carry a buck knife back then. Had it on my belt in a leather sheath. This thing was dull as hell; I'd been using it to strip wires and pry open busted amps. But, without even thinking about it, I pulled out that knife and I stabbed my girl in the ass. Right up the old poop-chute.

"Startled her something fierce, I suppose, because she tensed up and bit down hard. Cut his dick off with her teeth. It was a two-fer!"

Ben gagged. The wracking dry heaves threw his weight forward, pulling on the screws in his hands, making them ooze fresh blood.

"Stupidly, I called the cops. Told them I caught my cheatin' girl with a man and lost my shit. They put me away for seven years. Both of 'em survived, though she always walked funny after, and I'm betting he didn't have much of a life without his prick. Anyway, the upshot is I didn't get a murder rap. Would've been in a lot longer if they hadn't lived.

"In prison, I learned a lot of interesting stuff. Things like, how to hide a dead body, you know? I also learned that I wanted to do it again. Do violence to another human being, I mean. It's, I don't know, *electric*.

"And, when I got out, the god damn horticulturist was living in my house. She was the first one I brought down here."

On the workbench, Leeza groaned. Her head lolled and she regarded Ben through slitted eyes. He gave her a weak smile.

"It's okay, baby. We're gonna be okay."

She tried to smile back, but Manny moved into view. He flashed his dentures at her.

"No, you're not."

Whirling away from her, Manny once again retrieved the box cutter. He whicked away the edges of Ben's underwear, cutting his hips on both sides in the process.

Ben was no longer hard.

Manny pulled open the drawer that had the WD-40 in it. He rattled around in there for a bit and came up with a monkey wrench. Opening it wide as he crossed back to Ben, he whistled an old Stones tune.

"I'm not gonna say I feel bad about what I did to your woman. I don't. However, I do feel a strong sense of fair play. Tit for tat, if you will. Since I hurt her pretty bad in her sexy place, I'm gonna do the same for you, Benny."

"Don't. Please. You don't have to."

Manny tsked.

"There's where you're wrong, boy. The scales always need to be balanced. I jacked up her *yin* so I'm gonna have to hurt your *yang*. Just how it goes."

He slid the edges of the wrench over one of Ben's testicles.

"Oh, Jesus, no. Not that. Please, Manny. I'm begging you."

Manny stopped. He looked up at his face.

"I do believe you just used the Lord's name in vain, Benny. There may be hope for you yet."

With his big knuckles flexing, Manny tightened the threads of the monkey wrench. With agonizing slowness, the two rusty steel ends cinched together.

"No no no nonononononono…"

Ben stopped speaking. His mouth cracked open in a wide "O". A mouse squeak eased from his throat.

Manny tightened.

The ball popped.

Ben screamed. It went on and on. The backs of his knees slammed into the wall as he tried to run away from the pain. He pissed himself, hot urine and blood ran down his legs, over the screw in his feet to puddle on the floor.

"Yup. That'll do ya for a while. I think it's the lady's turn again." He looked Leeza up and down, put a hand idly on one of her breasts. "Almost a shame to mess up such perfect tits. But, you know what? Maybe I'll just keep 'em after your dead. Mount 'em to a plaque and just play with 'em whenever I want."

Manny tightened the monkey wrench as he moved it closer to her nipple. He hummed that Stones song again.

Behind him, Ben thrashed against the screws holding his hands in place. Blood pulsed out around them and ran down his forearms to drip from his elbows. Gritting his teeth, he kept at it, working his hands over the end of the screws.

Manny blew on her nipple until it grew hard, straining upward, like it wanted to be kissed. Gently, he positioned the wrench, checking the width.

"Still too much. Have to tighten down a bit, my dear. Hope you don't mind."

He twisted a tiny bit at a time, eyeing the gap as it closed on the protruding nipple.

"Almost there."

A wet, tearing sound accompanied by a grunt of pain from behind distracted him. He started to turn and Ben landed on him, bloody, clawed hands scrambling for purchase on the old man's clothes.

Manny went over, dropping the wrench. For half a second, it hung from her nipple, stretching her breast sideways. Then, it fell, glancing off Manny's forehead.

"Ow," he said.

"Fuck you, you horrible geezer psycho son-of-a-bitch." It all came out at once, almost one word. Manny laughed, fighting him off. Ben's feet were still screwed down.

"Benjamin," Manny snorted. "Language."

Ben got his fingers around Manny's throat. He squeezed. Blood seeped from the holes in the back of hands.

"Die, motherfucker."

Manny's voice was starting to sound a little hoarse. He pulled against Ben's hands, but Ben had leverage. Still, Manny squeaked out a few words.

"Wow. When you start swearing, you really run with it."

"Just *die*."

Manny gave up pulling on Ben's hands. From next to his head, he grabbed the fallen monkey wrench. His voice was a barely audible croak.

"No."

Manny smashed the wrench against Ben's already abused head.

Ben scrambled away, but was brought up short by his tethered feet.

Manny brought the wrench down on Ben's leg, shattering the kneecap.

Ben fell sideways with a shocked whimper.

"You're no match for me, boy," Manny said in a sandpaper voice.

Sidling over to Ben, Manny raised the wrench high.

Ben lunged, punching Manny in the gut, leaning into it. Manny shook his head. He lowered the wrench, shook his head.

"That didn't even hurt, Ben. You're pathetic, you know that? A total pussy."

Ben, still touching Manny's gut, yanked across and backward. In his hand, he held the box cutter. Both men looked down. A wide fissure opened in Manny's shirt, and in the flesh beneath. The wound revealed an inch-deep gully of ugly, yellow fat. Blood welled in the groove, then spilled out. It quickly soaked Manny's shirt, spilled over his belt and stained his corduroy pants.

"Well, fuck me," he said. He dropped the wrench with a clatter.

"Yeah," Ben said. "Fuck you."

Ben held Manny by the collar. He stared into the other man's eyes and watched them lose focus. Finally, the old man stopped breathing.

Ben slid the blade of the box cutter into Manny's throat, severing the carotid artery. Blood oozed from it like maple sap. Ben stabbed him again, just to be sure.

Pushing the dead man aside, Ben did a sit-up to reach his ankles. He cut the cord binding them. Then he retrieved the drill, thankfully still within reach. Deliberately avoiding looking at the bloody end of it, he set it to "reverse". He clenched his jaw as he withdrew the drywall screw from the beam, from his feet.

On his knees, he crawled to the workbench. He cut the clothesline holding one leg, then the other. She put her legs together and pulled her knees to her chest.

He painfully made his way to the other end of the bench, still not looking at his wife. He cut the cord from her wrists. She lay up there, in the fetal position, silently crying.

He set down the blade. He eased himself to a standing position, on the balls of his feet. The holes in them stretched painfully. He stroked Leeza's hair with one bloody hand.

"We're going to be okay. We're alive. It's our house now."

She looked at him with dead eyes.

"You promised not to swear."

He barked a single, sharp laugh.

"Well, shit, honey. There were extenuating circumstances, you know?"

The following Monday, the police dug up the backyard. The remains of nine people were buried there.

Leeza had reconstructive surgery to repair the damage inside her. The doctor assured them she could have a normal sex life once she'd healed completely.

The doctor was wrong. Physically, she recovered completely, but she would never have sex again.

Their marriage lasted another year. They rarely spoke, avoided eye contact and slept in separate rooms. One unremarkable morning, over coffee, she told him she wanted a divorce. He simply nodded.

He got the house. She didn't want it. Eventually, he put in a pool.

Every few months, he would go down to the room. He would close the door and stand in the profound silence. He would see flashes of the carnage, hear the screaming. He would feel Manny's hot blood pouring over his hand.

After a couple years, he started dating Marnia, a bartender at an upscale restaurant downtown. She was pretty. He watched her eyes, to see if she looked at other men. He almost *wanted* her to stray. So he could catch her. Punish them both.

And, if something happened, if he got carried away. Well, there were vacant lots not too far away. And, of course, his cousin owned a Bobcat.

Bio

Ken has been writing professionally for about six years. His work has appeared in dozens of anthologies and magazines, and the occasional podcast. He has two story collections, *An Aberrant Mind*, and *Sex, Gore, & Millipedes*. He edits an annual themed anthology (Recurring Nightmares) for the Great Lakes Association of Horror Writers. Ken is an Affiliate member of HWA. He has also written TV commercials, sketch comedy, a music video, and a zombie movie. Recently, he co-wrote a novel (likely out by Summer 2017), and they are working on the sequel.

When not writing, Ken drives the bookmobile for his local library. He lives with his family and three cats, one of whom is dead but we don't hold that against her.

You can connect with him via social media on the following platforms: Website:
http://ken-macgregor.com
Twitter: @kenmacgregor
Facebook:https://www.facebook.com/KenMacGregorAuthor
Pinterest: https://www.pinterest.com/macgregorken/

Dragon's Roost Press is the fever dream brainchild of dark speculative fiction author Michael Cieslak. Since 2014, their goal has been to find the best speculative fiction authors and share their work with the public. For more information about Dragon's Roost Press and their publications, please visit: http://thedragonsroost.net/styled-3/index.html.

Also Available from Dragon's Roost Press

Robotic Animals
Televisions Which Reveal Alternate Universes
Inanimate Objects Brought to Life
People Struggling to Survive in Apocalyptic Wastelands
Sentient Cutlery

and much, much more

Desolation: 21 Tales for Tails is a collection of dark speculative fiction whose stories all focus on themes of loneliness, isolation, and abandonment.

Enter into strange worlds envisioned by some of the most inventive writing today.

Combine the mind splintering horror of the Cthulhu Mythos and the heart shattering portion of that most terrible of emotions -- love -- and what do you have? You have *Eldritch Embraces: Putting the Love Back in Lovecraft.*

This collection of short stories from some of the best authors working in the fields of horror and dark speculative fiction blends romance and Lovecraft in a way which will make you sigh, smile, weep, or leave you the hollow shell of your former self.

A portion of the proceeds of each sale of *Desolation: 21 Tales for Tails* and *Eldritch Embraces: Putting the Love Back in Lovecraft* benefit the Last Day Dog Rescue Organization.

Also Available from Dragon's Roost Press

The Maiden's Courage

by Mary Lynne Gibbs

The best man on the pirate ship is a girl named Alex.

Alexandra "Alex" Gardner is the reluctant cabin boy on *The Bloody Maiden*, a ruthless pirate ship run by the charmingly evil Captain Montgomery. The crew is convinced she's a boy, and she hopes it stays that way until she has the chance to avenge the deaths of her mother and brother at the hands of the crew. All goes well until the ship takes a handsome captive. Could her feelings for him ruin her charade?

Sebastian Whitley is a young man in love. He sails on his father's ship, trying to find the beautiful girl he's lost. When he's captured by *The Bloody Maiden*, the annoying cabin boy saves his life – and makes it more difficult at the same time. His savior is actually a girl, and if Sebastian doesn't keep quiet, it could mean both their deaths.

Together, they have to thwart a mutiny, get revenge, and get off the ship before Alex's secret is revealed. If not, it's the plank for both of them.

Also Available from Dragon's Roost Press

Jericho Rising

by Mary Lynne Gibbs

In post-World War III, small town Michigan, a self-proclaimed, violent, and insane High Priestess has taken control, reducing the remaining men to nothing more than slaves and playthings.

Jericho, the reluctant leader of the Resistance, must fight her own family to preserve the freedom and equality of all in her care – male and female alike. She's torn between love and duty, and with traitors around every corner, she has no idea who to trust anymore.

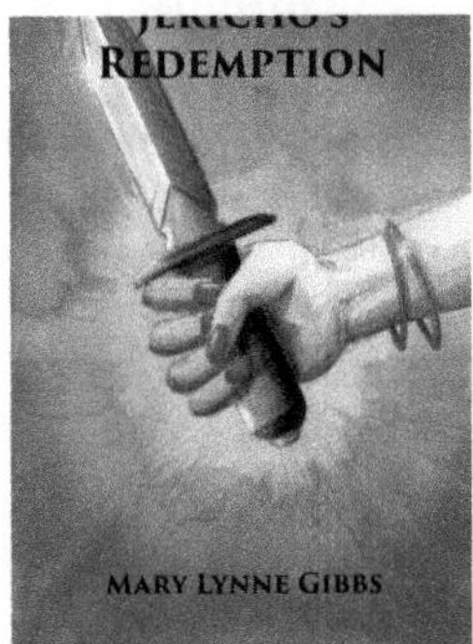

Jericho's Redemption

by Mary Lynne Gibbs

The battle is over, but the war has just begun. Jericho returns to the Obsidian camp, only to learn that her sister Candace destroyed it as part of a plot to dismantle the resistance movement that brought down their mother, the High Priestess. The rest of the resistance blames Jericho for the deaths of their friends, but that's the least of her worries. Not only does Jericho now have to right the wrongs her sister has done, she must contend with a few guests to the camp who bring secrets that will change her life forever. Either she'll redeem herself in the eyes of her comrades, or she'll die trying.

Also Available from Dragon's Roost Press

Hell Hath No Fury

by Peggy Christie

Ever wonder how you might handle a sabbatical from work? Think the bible told you everything there is to know about the Devil? What if the noises coming from under your child's bed weren't just in his imagination?

Crack open Hell Hath No Fury, a collection of 21 tales of horror and dark fiction, to learn the answers to these questions. Discover stories of psychotic delusions, ghosts, a murder victim's revenge, and a family brought closer together through torture. All of this and more awaits inside the book you hold in your hands right now.

Printed in the USA
CPSIA information can be obtained
at www.ICGtesting.com
LVHW080245161123
763892LV00063B/1327